Amy Cross is the author of more than 100 horror, paranormal, fantasy and thriller novels.

OTHER TITLES
BY AMY CROSS INCLUDE

American Coven
Asylum
B&B
The Body at Auercliff
The Bride of Ashbyrn House
The Devil, the Witch and the Whore
Devil's Briar
The Dog
Eli's Town
The Farm
The Ghosts of Lakeforth Hotel
The Girl Who Never Came Back
Haunted
The Haunting of Blackwych Grange
The Night Girl
The Nurse
Other People's Bodies
Perfect Little Monsters & Other Stories
The Printer From Hell
The Shades
Tenderling
Twisted Little Things & Other Stories
The Vampire of Downing Street & Other Stories
Ward Z

Annie's Room

AMY CROSS

First published by Dark Season Books,
United Kingdom, 2017

Copyright © 2017 Amy Cross

All rights reserved. This book is a work of fiction. Names, characters, places, incidents and businesses are the product of the author's imagination or are used fictitiously. Any resemblance to actual persons, living or dead, or to actual events or locates, is entirely coincidental.

ISBN: 9781521242254

Also available in e-book format.

www.amycross.com

CONTENTS

PROLOGUE
PAGE 1

CHAPTER ONE
PAGE 5

CHAPTER TWO
PAGE 18

CHAPTER THREE
PAGE 25

CHAPTER FOUR
PAGE 35

CHAPTER FIVE
PAGE 40

CHAPTER SIX
PAGE 50

CHAPTER SEVEN
PAGE 58

CHAPTER EIGHT
PAGE 67

CHAPTER NINE
PAGE 76

CHAPTER TEN
PAGE 83

Chapter Eleven
page 94

Chapter Twelve
page 106

Chapter Thirteen
page 118

Chapter Fourteen
page 125

Chapter Fifteen
page 130

Chapter Sixteen
page 141

Chapter Seventeen
page 147

Chapter Eighteen
page 153

Chapter Nineteen
page 159

Chapter Twenty
page 189

Epilogue
page 192

ANNIE'S ROOM

PROLOGUE

THROWING MYSELF THROUGH THE open doorway, I land hard on the porch and let out a cry of pain as I feel something snapping in my chest.

Probably just another rib.

I haul myself up, pushing past the pain in my abdomen as I start dragging myself toward the top of the steps. My legs, encased in the plaster casts, are starting to ache but I don't have time to stop. When I get to the first step, I heave myself over the edge and then try to protect my head as I rattle down and slam into the mud at the bottom. I catch one of my legs in the process, but the pain is secondary as I start pulling myself across the garden, desperate to get away from the house. Rain is falling all around, filling the night air with a constant, growing hiss.

Digging my fingers into the mud, I try to pull myself along, only for my hands to slip. I try again, and this time I'm able to get a few feet further. Out of breath and shivering cold as mud soaks through my shirt, I look forward for a moment, but with no moonlight to guide me, all I can see is the row of dark trees at the far end of the garden, marking the start of the forest. I reach out and dig my right hand deeper into the mud, and once I'm sure I've got a decent grip I try pulling myself along.

I have to stop after a moment. The pain in my abdomen is immense now, filling the left side of my body with a throbbing ache that's at once both numbing and agonizing. Barely able to breathe, I take several deep, hawking gulps of air, but I feel as if something is partially blocking my airway, most likely as a result of the tumble down the stairs. Realizing that I need to find some more strength from somewhere, I take a few more breaths before turning and looking over my shoulder, back toward the dark house.

She's there.

Standing in the doorway, barely visible, her silhouette is just about visible. A moment later, she steps out through the broken door and onto the porch, and although I can't make out any of her features, I know it's her and I know she's coming from me.

"Mom!" I scream. "Help me!"

I turn and start dragging myself further across the mud. Every second feels like it might be my last, as if I might collapse, but each time I manage to find some more strength from somewhere. My body body is wracked with pain now, and I can feel cold mud seeping under the edge of my plaster casts and dribbling down to my knees. Heaving myself onward, I try to summon the energy to get a little further, but finally I drop down hard against the mud, some of which splashes into my open mouth. Crying out, I spit the mud away as I raise my face into the rain, and a moment later I realize I can feel someone getting closer.

I turn and see that the figure has come down off the porch now and is following me across the mud.

"Leave me alone!" I shout, with tears running down my cheeks. "What do you want from me?"

Turning, I continue to drag myself away from the house. I know it's hopeless, I know she'll catch me, but I have to keep trying. Sobbing but somehow managing to continue, I reach out and rig my hands once more into the mud, pressing the fingers deep into the sludgy mix in the hope that I might gain a better hold, and then I let out a cry of pain as I manage to drag myself a couple more feet. I quickly do the same again, feeling the cold mud against my belly as rain pounds down onto my back. Stopping for a moment, I feel for a few brief seconds as if I should just give up and accept what comes, but that sensation quickly subsides and instead I reach out, grabbing more mud and hauling myself forward, and then I reach out again...

Only this time, my right hand pushes down into the mud and finds something a little way beneath the surface. Something cold, and hard like... bone. I feel my fingers slipping into two sockets, and my thumb presses against a series of coarse, raised bumps that can only be teeth. I freeze, telling myself that I have to be wrong, before finally using my left hand to drag myself forward as I raise my right hand from the mud. My fingers are still pushed deep into the sockets of the human skull, and

I stare in horror as I watch rain lashing down, washing mud from the bony surface and from my hand too, revealing the dead face staring back at me.

Suddenly the cold, which had been soaking through my shirt already, becomes much, much colder, as if it the mud and rain has found a way to penetrate my skin and soak down to my bones. I stare in horror at the skull in my right hand, but although I want to cry out and throw it to one side, I can't manage to make my fingers obey. All I can do is crawl closer until I'm staring directly into the skull's eyes, and then I set it down in the mud and finally manage to let go. Rain pours down onto us both, washing away more flecks of dirt from the skull until it stares back at me.

Sensing movement nearby, I slowly turn and look up. The dark figure from the house is now standing directly behind, looking straight down at me.

CHAPTER ONE

Five days earlier

"YOU JUST HAD TO do it *this* week, didn't you?" Mom sighs as she switches off the ignition. "Both legs, on the exact same day we were scheduled to move house."

"I'm sorry," I tell her for the hundredth – no, the *thousandth* – time. "I didn't exactly fall off my bike on purpose."

She turns to me, and although she's clearly annoyed, there's still a weary smile that lets me know I'm not really in trouble. "On the plus side," she mutters, "spending so much time with you at the hospital meant I could leave the actual moving work to your father and Scott, so I guess I shouldn't complain too much." She looks down at my legs, both of which are encased in plaster from just above the knee all the way down to the ankle. "And you didn't 'fall' off your bike, Annie, you *flew* off it. At speed. Into the side of a truck." She reaches over and ruffles my hair. "For God's sake, you could have been killed."

"I'm sorry." Glancing out the window, I see the new house towering high above the driveway, and I'm immediately struck by how dark and brooding the place looks. Seriously, it's as if my parents set out to find a house that would drive visitors away. The wooden walls are gray and worn, as if the place hasn't been renovated since the year zero. "Is this it?" I ask, keen to change the subject. "What are we, The Addams Family?"

"It's a lovely house," she replies, opening the door and stepping out of the car before heading around to the trunk so she can take out the fold-up wheelchair. "It just needs some care and attention, that's all. Would you rather live in some soulless, airless modern construction?"

"Yes."

"Tough."

"And we're out in the middle of nowhere," I mutter, turning and looking back along the barren driveway. "We're miles from civilization. The nearest house is, what, five miles away? Ten? What exactly am I supposed to do all summer, commune with nature?"

"First you'll have to get your legs healed," she replies, setting the wheelchair next to the car. "Until then, you know what the doctor said."

"Yeah, but we're not actually going to listen to him, are we?" I say with a smile, before realizing that she's serious. "Mom? No way, I can't *actually* be confined to bed!"

"It's an essential part of your recovery."

"But -"

"No buts," she adds. "Annie Riley, you're going to follow the doctor's orders to the letter, and that means resting in bed while your legs heal. You'll be up and about eventually, but these things take time and if you don't like that, I only have one piece of advice for you."

"What's that?" I ask, feeling a sense of doom as I look back up at the house.

"Don't break your legs again," she continues, reaching into the car and patting my shoulder. "Now let's try to figure out how to get you into this wheelchair. Your father's inside, maybe I should go and get him to help. I'm not quite sure how we're going to get you upstairs."

"Upstairs?" I reply, my eyes widening with shock. "You have to be joking!"

She sighs. "Annie -"

"You can't put me upstairs! That's insane! I have to be downstairs!"

"There's no room," she explains, already sounding as if she's ready to drop. "Annie, please... Once you're up there, it'll be fine. I know it's not ideal, but your father and I have talked it over and it's really the only way we can manage."

She pauses, watching me with a hint of concern.

"You know we won't just stick you up there and forget about you, right?" she asks finally, forcing a faint smile that in no way hides her frazzled exhaustion. "Trust me, after a few hours you'll be *begging* us to leave you in peace!"

"Great," I mutter, looking down at my useless, plaster-clad legs, "I guess summer's canceled. I probably won't see the outside world again until winter."

***

"And this is your room!" Dad says proudly, pushing the door open and wheeling me into a small, undecorated space on the top floor. "What do you think?"

"I think there's been some kind of mistake," I reply. "My name is Annie Riley and I live in New York. I'm not a country bumpkin."

"That's the spirit."

"There's mold," I point out, sniffing the air.

"There's no mold."

"I can see it. Over there, by the window, there's mold growing up from the floor."

"That's just some old wallpaper," he replies, wheeling me to the side of the bare, metal-framed bed. Reaching over to the wall, he scratches at the mold, causing some of it to flake off. He takes a sniff of his fingers and immediately recoils, clearly disgusted. "Well, whatever, I'll get rid of it. It's not the dangerous kind of mold."

"Can you at least open the window?" I ask. "I'm worried about fumes."

"There's not *that* much of it," he says, although he opens the window as far as it'll go before coming back to my wheelchair. "It's an old house, you have to expect certain... unusual features. One of the reasons we moved all the way out here was to get away from the sterilized apartments of the city and give you kids a chance to explore the real world."

"I *liked* the sterilized apartments of the city," I tell him, wincing slightly as he reaches around from behind and takes hold of me, ready to lift me onto the bed. "I was very comfortable in the sterilized apartments of the city. I liked not having random patches of dirt and straw in the corner of my room."

"Huh?" He looks over at the far corner. "I'll get rid of that too."

It only takes a few seconds for him to lift me from the chair and set me on the bed, and when he asks if the move hurt my legs at all, I lie: I tell him I'm fine, that they don't hurt, and that he should stop fussing. The truth, however, is that as he gently lifts my plaster-clad legs onto the bed and then wheels the chair to the corner, I feel like a prisoner who's being placed in a new cell. Sure, that might be a slight over-reaction, but back in New York I had a whole city on my doorstep, and now all I have is a window that offers a fine view of some distant trees. Plus, the air smells clean, and I'm not used to that at all.

"You're not stuck in bed forever," Dad says, grabbing a hold-all from the floor and setting it next to me on the bed. "Three or four weeks, tops, provided you actually cooperate."

"And then we can move back to New York?"

"And then you'll be up and about, and you can explore Dunceford."

"Dunceford," I mutter with a sigh. "Even the name..."

"You've got rolling countryside for miles in every direction," he continues. "Fields, fresh air, a forest... I'd have given anything to grow up in a place like this. You're fifteen years old, Annie, you should learn to get about in the natural world."

"But what if I've evolved to *need* smog?" I ask. "What if my body has become optimized to city living and I end up dying in a clean environment? What if clean, fresh air is actually toxic to me? That's a very real possibility that no-one seems to be considering."

"Plus, you have this." He slides my laptop from the bag and places it on my lap. "I made sure it wasn't buried away in one of the packing crates when we arrived yesterday."

"Thanks," I reply, opening the lid and hitting the power button.

"And we should have internet by Wednesday next week."

I smile, amused by the joke, before turning to him as I realize he might be serious. "What?"

"They have to lay some new cables or something."

I'm trying not to panic, but... "We have no internet?"

"Relax," he says with a smile, "it *is* possible to live without being online."

"But -" Staring at my laptop as it powers up, I suddenly feel as if I've been ripped away from the real world and dropped into the Dark Ages. No streaming music, no streaming video, no ebooks or websites, no instant chat, no social media, no news, no forums, no access to my short stories and other stuff in the cloud. I swear to God, I feel like I might actually burst into tears.

"We have DVDs," he adds. "I'll bring some up."

"DVDs?" I reply. "What is this, the Victorian age?"

"The house is older than that, actually," he explains, heading to the door. "Sorry, Annie, I know it's not exactly ideal to spend your first weeks here in bed, but if you hadn't fallen off your bike -"

"I know," I reply, trying and failing to hide my irritability. "It's all my fault that I'm bedridden." Sighing, I close the laptop lid. I can tell I'm coming across as some kind of bratty teenager, and I don't like it. "And I'm sure I'll thank you and Mom for moving us out here eventually," I continue with another sigh. "I'm sure I'll learn to love it here, I just have to adjust to the change of pace. And I need to be able to -"

I look over at the door, suddenly aware that someone was watching us. Whoever it was, they've slipped out of sight before I get to see them, but I figure it was probably my dumb little brother.

"I need to be able to walk again," I add, turning back to Dad. "That's what I need the most."

"I'll bring some more things up as we unpack," he replies. "Hold tight, it's going to be great in this new house, I promise."

I nod, but as soon as he's left the room I find myself sitting on the bed with no idea what to do next. My phone was lost in the bike accident and I still don't have a new one, and now the lack of internet means I'm cut off from the world. Sitting up a little more, I crane my neck and look out the window, but all I manage to see if the trees that line the far end of the lawn. I know it's great to 'connect' with the natural world and all that stuff, but still, a short vacation would have been enough. I really don't get why we had to move hundreds of miles and come live in the sticks. Still, it'd be a lot better if I wasn't confined to bed, and that part at least I all my fault.

Damn me.

Feeling an itch around my right knee, I look around for my scratcher before realizing that Mom and Dad forgot to bring it up for me. When I try to slip a finger under the plaster cast, I realize that there's no way I can reach the itch without help, although I try digging my finger deeper and I swear I'm *almost* there...

Hearing a bump nearby, I turn and once again see a faint shape slipping out of view in the doorway.

"Scott," I say, not amused, "can you go get my scratcher from Mom and Dad?"

I wait.

No reply.

He's blatantly out there on the landing, but I guess he thinks he's being funny.

"Scott, can you cut the games and just fetch my scratcher? Please?"

Nothing.

"Damn it," I mutter, leaning back on the bed as I try to banish the itch using the power of my mind. I have no idea how I'm going to survive being holed up in this room for a couple of weeks, but if I'm to stand any chance at all, I *need* a scratcher to deal with the itches under my plaster casts. The worst part is, this really *is* all my fault. If I hadn't come off my bike last week, I'd be able to go explore the new area, and that *would* be kind of neat.

Instead I'm stuck here, in this bare little room, listening to the sound of my family unpacking boxes in the room below.

***

"You guys didn't have to eat up here in my room with me," I tell them later, as I take another slice of pizza off the plate, "but... Thanks."

"We couldn't leave you up here by yourself," Mom points out. She, Dad and Scott are sitting on uncomfortable-looking wooden chairs next to my bed, and they've set up a camp table to hold the pizza and soda bottles. It's actually kind of cute. "It would've been sad to be eating downstairs while knowing you're up here alone."

"It'd be funny," Scott mutters with a grin.

"Maybe I could get up a little," I suggest. "I mean, I'm not crippled, I just have these casts on and we have those crutches..."

"You saw the stairs, honey," Dad replies. "Even *with* crutches, you'd have trouble maneuvering. Besides, the doctor said you need to stay in bed and let your legs heal properly. That was a condition of letting you out so soon, remember? He actually wanted to keep you in until the weekend."

"Sure," I reply, "but -"

"But nothing. Be a good patient."

"I just don't know what I'm going to *do* all day," I reply, looking over at the window. Night has fallen outside, and after just one afternoon and evening of being in this room, I'm already starting to go stir crazy. My laptop is useless without an internet connection, and Mom still hasn't managed to find any of the boxes with my books. "Seriously," I continue, turning back to them, "what am I going to do tomorrow? I'll be here in this room all day, and you guys are going to be busy, so what am I going to *do*?"

"Scott'll come and keep you company," Mom suggests.

"No," Scott and I say at the same time, before he adds: "No way. I want to explore the forest. It looks cool out there."

"I'm going to turn into an old crone," I mutter. "I'll just waste away in this room and -"

Suddenly there's a loud bang from downstairs, followed by a thud and then another bang. We all turn and look over at the door, and after a moment I look back at Mom and Dad and see the concern in their eyes.

"What was that?" I ask cautiously. "Do I have another sibling you guys have been hiding from me?"

"I..." Dad pauses, before getting to his feet. He steps on the particularly loose, particularly annoying floorboard next to my bed as he heads out to the landing, where he stops for a moment. "It was nothing. Probably just the wind blowing a door shut."

"I thought we locked the front door?" Mom says.

"A window, then." He pauses again. "I'll go take

a look. Don't worry, it's nothing."

He walks out of view, and a moment later I hear him making his way down the creaking stairs.

"That was *not* nothing," I say finally, turning to Mom. "That was, like, something."

"It was probably the wind," she replies, not entirely convincingly.

Looking over at the window, I can just about see the tops of the trees against the dark sky. "There's no wind out there," I say after a moment. "It's completely still." Turning to her, I can still see the hint of worry in her eyes as we all listen to the sound of Dad moving about downstairs. I swear, every floorboard in this house seems designed to make the maximum possible amount of noise when it's stepped on.

"What if it's a ghost?" Scott whispers.

"There are no ghosts here," Mom tells him.

"But what if there are?"

"Don't be stupid," I reply, before turning to look over at Mom. "Tell him. There are no ghosts here, right?"

"There are no ghosts here," she says, ruffling the top of his head with her right hand. "Come on, let's not get spooked. Something probably fell over, that's all." She turns to me. "You should see what it's like down there, we've got packing crates everywhere, we've got things propped against other things, it's going to take days before we're all settled in. I never knew we had so much stuff until we had to move it out here. We should have taken the opportunity to de-clutter, but -"

She stops speaking as we all hear Dad coming

back up the stairs. A moment later he appears in the doorway.

"I couldn't see anything," he says. "All the doors and windows are locked, so I guess something just tipped over." He breathes a sigh of relief as he comes back into the room and sits down, but he seems a little stiff and awkward, less relaxed than a couple of minutes ago. "Come on, guys, it's a new house, let's not go spooking ourselves. I don't know about the rest of you, but I'm starting to think about hitting the sack after dinner. It's been a long day, and we've got so much to do tomorrow."

"Lucky you," I mutter.

"You'll be up and about in no time," Mom reminds me. "Who wants the last slice of pizza?"

"Me!" Scott snaps, grabbing the slice and licking the top, which is his customary way of claiming food and ensuring that no-one tries to take it away from him. With a satisfied grin, he takes a bite.

Looking down at the bare plate, with just a few crumbs left in the middle, I realize with a heavy heart that soon everyone's going to go back downstairs and start getting ready for bed, and I'm going to be left here in my room until they get up again in the morning. I know I shouldn't start feeling sorry for myself, and I know that in normal circumstances I'd *want* to be alone in my room, but I'd at least like to have the *option* of getting out of bed. Besides, this isn't *my* room, not really. It feels more like we've checked into a rotten, rundown hotel.

"You look sad," Mom says suddenly, placing a

hand on my knee. "Don't be sad, Annie. You'll be -"

"Up and about in no time," I reply, "yeah, people keep saying that." I pause, before looking over at the empty doorway. For a moment, I feel a shiver run down my spine at the thought that someone was out there just now, watching us, but I figure I'm just letting my imagination get cranked up early. "And promise me there are no ghosts," I mutter, turning to Mom. "Do we even know anything about the people who lived in this house before us?"

"Nothing," Dad interjects, a little too quickly. "Come on, don't worry about it."

"Fine," I reply. "I just don't want them haunting us. Whoever they were, this is our house now, not theirs."

CHAPTER TWO

Seventy-one years ago

FATHER IS BEATING MOTHER again tonight. I can hear their argument from my room, although in truth it's not much of an argument at all; Father is simply telling Mother her inadequacies and pressing home his point with his fists.

As usual, she brought it on herself.

Their voices aren't raised at all. I can hear Father's voice rumbling along, and then there are the occasional low bumps and impacts, which I know are the moments when he pushes her or hits her. Sometimes, I even hear the sound of a table being pushed aside, as if perhaps she's trying to hide, and a few minutes ago there was a shudder that rattled the glass in my bedroom window. That's when I know he's really hurting her. When the whole house shakes.

Of course, if she'd just stay still and take the

punishment she's earned, I'd have more respect for her.

I stay on my bed, of course. I know better than to get involved. Besides, Mother is used to such things, so she knows how to handle herself. Sometimes I think that even though she has been married to Father for two decades, I at just sixteen years of age already have a better understanding of how to avoid the brunt of his temper. Why does she not learn? Why does she do things that she knows will earn his ire? If I were her, I would not suffer such beatings, but it's almost as if she *wants* to push him like this. I'm not excusing Father, of course, not for one moment; what he does is in some ways horrible and wrong, but it's also necessary. Mother could avoid his temper if she was smarter.

When I'm older and have a husband, *I* shall be smarter.

The house falls quiet a little before midnight, and eventually I hear footsteps coming up. From the pattern of the footfall, and also from experience of these matters, I know full well that its Mother who is retiring to bed. After a beating, she always stays down in the room with Father for a while, for at least an hour, before coming upstairs. I never understand what goes on in that silent hour, but perhaps he instructs her to stay, or perhaps she simply wishes to wait and let things get back to normal. I wish I could ask her, but I cannot.

A moment later, she appears in the doorway, watching me.

"I'm not asleep," I tell her from the darkness.

"You should be," she replies, her voice weak and hurt. "It's late."

"I'm sorry."

"Did you hear -" She pauses.

I choose not to answer.

"You'll be working with Father again tomorrow," she continues. "He wants to teach you about the garden."

"As you wish."

"It's good for you to learn," she adds. "Father says you're to help him with some important work. He says you'll learn more with him for a few days than you'd learn in a month at school."

"I'm sure he's right," I say after a moment.

She murmurs her agreement, and then she seems to loiter for a few seconds, as if there's something else she wants to say, before she turns and makes her way to the other bedroom. I wait and listen until I hear the door quietly swinging shut, and then I wait a moment longer until I feel that it's safe to get out of bed. The loose floorboard next to my bed shifts and creaks slightly. Heading to the door, I lean out to the landing and check that the coast is clear, before avoiding all the creaking floorboards on the way to the top of the stairs. I can hear Mother sobbing softly in my parents' bedroom, which means that there's no chance of her coming out for a while. That's good. I start making my way down the dark stairs until I reach the hallway and see the light of a single candle flickering in the front room.

When I get to the next doorway, I pause for a moment and watch Father as he raises a glass to his lips and takes a sip of whiskey. He's such a still and calm man at the best of times, but doubly so after an altercation with Mother. Disciplining her must be so tiring for him, both mentally and physically. The candlelight casts his constantly shifting shadow against the far wall, and it's clear that he's deep, deep in thought. Some people say that Father is a brutish man, but they don't see him the way I see him. They don't see the great intelligence in his eyes, and they never see him like this, contemplating life as he sits in his armchair before bed.

I take a step forward.

The floorboard creaks beneath my left foot.

I stop.

Father stares down at his glass for a moment, before turning his head slightly. Not enough to look directly at me, mind, but enough to indicate that he knows I'm here. The candlelight catches the side of his face, picking out his strong, firm brow and his high cheekbones, and then he raises his glass and finishes the rest of his whiskey.

My cue.

"Shall I refill that for you?" I ask, making my way over to him.

He doesn't reply, but when I try to take the glass from his hand, he lets me.

I head to the table in the far corner, where Father's drinks are kept. Holding his glass up, I see his fingerprints on the glass as well as smudges left by his lips. I give the glass a quick wipe with the sleeve of my dress, using just a little saliva to help the job, before setting the glass down and filling it from the bottle. It's in these small, quiet moments that I feel most comfortable, since at least I know precisely what I should be doing. I want to be useful; more than anything else in the world, I feel it is every human being's duty to be useful to someone else. Turning, I make my way back to Father's armchair and hold the glass out for him, and after a moment he takes it from my hand.

As he sips, I take a seat on the floor next to his chair. There's a stool nearby, as usual, but I never know if I'm allowed to sit there, and I feel as if he would have told me by now if that was the case. Perhaps it is for Mother, or perhaps he simply likes to keep it empty. Either way, the floor is perfectly comfortable, especially as I lean against the side of the chair and then rest my face against Father's leg. The smell of his trousers and the feel of the coarse fabric reminds me of childhood.

"Mother's gone to bed," he mutters finally, breaking the silence.

"I know," I reply, my voice tense with anticipation. I feel as if my chest is being drawn tight.

"She'll be up there for hours," he adds. "She won't be down 'til morning."

"I know." Glancing across the room, I see the darkness beyond the window. I can't see the edge of the forest, but I know it's out there in the cold night, and the thought makes me feel warmer here on the floor next to Father.

"She's a weak woman," he continues, before taking another sip of whiskey. "Not that that's a crime, it's in her nature, but still... She's weaker than most. You must mind not to let yourself become like her."

"She came to my room just now and told me that I must stay home for the rest of the week."

"That's right." He pauses. "Did she come *in* to your room?"

I nod, with my head still resting against his trouser leg.

"Did you invite her in," he asks, "or did she just enter of her own accord?"

I don't want to get Mother into more trouble, but at the same time I can't lie to Father. "She entered," I tell him, "of her own accord. Just a step or two, but she definitely entered."

"She'll have to be told about that, then," he mutters, sounding unimpressed. He takes another sip of whiskey. "That's *your* room, Annie, not hers. She has no right going in unless she's invited."

"I know."

"I'll tell her tomorrow."

"Thank you."

Reaching down, he puts a hand on the top of my head and ruffles my hair. When his fingers brush against my scalp, I can feel that his hand is unwashed after a hard day out in the garden, but I don't mind. It's good to have a little dirt in my hair, especially if that dirt comes to me via Father's touch, and I close my eyes so as to better enjoy the feel of him running his hand down to the back of my head and then onto the nape of my neck, where it rests for a moment, his fingertips pressing slightly against my flesh.

"There's going to have to be a change around here, Annie," he says finally. "Things have gone on this way long enough. It's not healthy."

I nod. His fingertips, still pressed against me,

remain in place. After a moment I turn my face slightly so that my cheek is more fully brushing against the side of Father's trousers. I breathe in deep, smelling that familiar mix of wood and smoke that comes only from Father at the end of a long day.

"A big change," he continues, although it's no longer clear whether he's talking to me or simply thinking out loud. "And I suppose I'll have to be the one who brings it about."

Turning, I look over at the dark window. Is she out there? Is she watching?

CHAPTER THREE

Today

I WAKE SUDDENLY, MY eyes flicking open in the dark room.

For a moment, I remain flat on my back, staring up at the ceiling. There's a cold draft coming through a gap at the edge of the window, blowing gently onto my shoulder. Listening to the silence of the house for a few seconds, I can't shake the distinct feeling that there was a noise just now, something that jolted me out of a dream.

Still, the house is quiet now.

I wait.

Silence.

With great difficulty, I use my elbows to haul myself up a little until I'm sitting in the bed. I turn and grab the window, pulling it down as hard as I can in an attempt to cut off the draft, but it's no use: when I hold a hand against the side, I can literally feel cool air coming through. That wouldn't happen in the city. I look out for a moment, and with the lights off in the room I'm able to see the garden below and the dark forest that starts a few hundred meters away. Having lived in New York all my life, I've never really *been* in a proper forest, and suddenly I'm struck by the sensation that something's out there, watching me. I know I'm just being dumb and letting my imagination run away with me, but still, the sense of isolation out here is pretty goddamn overpowering.

I really need to make sure I don't go nuts stuck here in this room over the next few weeks. I think maybe I could -

Suddenly I hear a creaking sound out on the landing.

Turning, I look over at my bedroom door, which I asked Mom to leave open. My room is dark but there's a patch of moonlight across the wall outside the door, and I listen for a moment until, after a few seconds, I hear another faint, cautious creak.

"Hey!" I hiss, keeping my voice low so I don't wake anyone up. "In here!"

I wait.

No reply.

"Mom, is that you? Dad?"

I wait again.

"Scott?"

Silence.

Frowning, I wait for another sound. Someone going into the bathroom, maybe, or footsteps heading downstairs to get a glass of water. It's our first night all together in the new house, so it figures that not everyone is sleeping so well. As the seconds tick by, however, I can't shake a growing sense of unease as I start to realize that whoever's out there, they seem to be just loitering on the landing, a little way out of sight.

"Scott?" I whisper, increasingly convinced that it must be my dumb little brother playing tricks. "Scott, come in here for a moment."

I wait.

"Scott," I continue, "I'm not in the mood for games, can you just get your ass in here?"

This time, after a couple of seconds, there's another faint creak, and it seems to be a little closer to the door.

"I'm wide awake," I add, "as you can tell. If you're going downstairs, can you get me something from the fridge? I don't care what, I'm just hungry."

I wait.

"Scott? Come on, don't be annoying, just go to the fridge for me and -"

Before I can finish, I see that something *is* moving outside my door. A shadow has began to edge into view across the patch of moonlight, which means that whoever's out there, they're standing in front of the window next to the top of the stairs, which in turn means that they've definitely heard me and are slowly inching toward my door.

"Scott?" I whisper again, determined not to let him know that he's freaking me out. It's just like him to try doing something like this on our first night here. "Listen," I continue, "I get it, you can't sleep so you want to bug me, but that's not really fair when I can't get you back. Either fetch me something from the fridge, or just go back to bed. I know it's boring here, but that doesn't mean you have to act like an idiot all the time." I wait for a reply. "Go and bug Mom and Dad, or -"

Suddenly there's a faint bump out on the landing, and the shadow pulls back out of view.

"Scott?"

Sighing, I wait for him to come back, but after several minutes have passed I realize he must have managed to get back to his room without making another sound.

"You're an ass-hat," I mutter, easing myself down onto my back and staring up at the ceiling. I know it's going to take a while to get back to sleep, but it's not like I have any other choice. I don't have any books up here yet and I can't even reach the light-switch, so all I can do is wait for tiredness to creep over me once again. After a few minutes, I hear another faint creak out on the landing, but this time I don't even bother to call out. If Scott wants to be an idiot, let him. I'll just wait until I eventually fall asleep and -

Suddenly the floorboard creaks right next to my bed.

I turn, but there's no-one there.

See? I'm already getting jumpy and Scott's definitely not helping. Taking a deep breath, I settle again and close my eyes. I have a feeling the next few weeks are going to be really goddamn tough.

***

"It's a new house," Mom replies the next morning as she uses a sponge and a bucket of warm water to help me wash on the bed. "I didn't sleep well either, I was tossing and turning all night."

"Can't you tell him to stay in his room?" I ask, raising my right arm so she can clean the pit. I hate being washed like this, like some kind of cripple, but at least it shouldn't take too long. Then again, I'm not really looking forward to seeing what the shower is like in this place, or trying to maneuver with my legs in plastic covers once I'm able to get around. "Either that, or chain him to his bed at night."

"He says he didn't get up."

"He's lying."

"Obviously, but..." She pauses as she dips the sponge into the bucket of water. "You know what Scott's like. You and he have always had something of an antagonistic relationship, and now he sees you as a sitting target. You need to get smarter and think of ways to stop him."

"I don't want to become his hobby," I reply firmly. "He's annoying enough as it is."

"I'll get your Dad to talk to him when he gets back from the store," she continues, moving the bucket away now that she's done. "Do you need the toilet?"

I shake my head.

"Be honest, Annie."

I pause, before nodding. Damn it, I hate being like this.

"I thought so," she replies, getting to her feet.

"I'll fetch the pan from downstairs."

"Do I really have to pee in a pan?" I ask, wincing at the very idea. After yesterday's attempts, I'm really not looking forward to feeling that cold steel again. "Can't I have, like, a catheter or something?"

"It's just for a few more weeks."

"It's humiliating."

"Don't you think you're overreacting just a little?" she replies, heading out the door. "Come on, you need to pee, you can't hold it in until you're on your feet again."

"Can you try to find some of my books?" I call after her. Hearing her heading down the stairs, I wait for a reply. "Mom? Can you try to find some of my books? Please?"

I wait, but I have no idea whether she heard me or not.

"I promise!" Scott calls out from somewhere else in the house, and a moment later I hear the back door opening.

Leaning on my left elbow, I turn and look out the window, and sure enough I see Scott racing across the garden, heading straight toward the forest. The way he's running, it's almost like he's mocking me, and for a moment I can't help feeling jealous. Damn it, I never thought I'd actually want to be out there scampering around in nature, but compared to being stuck in this bed, the idea seems positively -

And then I see her.

Over at the far end of the garden, a little way past the spot where Scott just ran, there's a woman in a white nightgown standing with her back to the house, seemingly looking down at a spot on the ground.

Squinting to get a better view, I keep expecting to suddenly realize that I'm wrong, that it's a trick of the light, but I feel a slow, creeping sense of fear as I realize that the woman is definitely there. From this angle, all I can tell is that she looks to be an adult and that she has dark, shoulder-length hair. I can't see anything on the ground in front of her, but she's just standing there, staring down as if something is really fascinating her. Looking over toward the trees, I realize that Scott is almost out of sight, and a moment later he disappears into the shadows. I turn back to look at the woman, but she's still just standing there, watching the ground.

"Annie's room," Mom says suddenly.

I turn to her and see that she's standing in the doorway, holding the metal pan as she runs a finger across part of the door jamb.

"I never noticed that before," she mutters with a frown.

"Mom, there's a woman outside," I reply, turning to look back out the window. "Do you -"

Stopping, I realize that the woman has disappeared. I look around, but there's no sign of her anywhere, not even when I crane my neck to look down at the yard immediately outside the back door. I swear I was only looking away for a few seconds, and it's hard to believe the woman could have got away unless she ran like hell. Oh God, I guess it's true: people in the countryside really *are* weird.

"I guess Scott must have done this," Mom

continues, before bringing the pan over to the bed. "Funny, I -"

"There was a woman out there," I tell her, still looking out the window. "Did you see her?"

"A woman out where?" She looks out at the garden for a moment. "I don't see anyone."

"She was right there," I reply, pointing to the spot about a hundred meters away from the back door where the woman was standing. "She was wearing a white dress and she had black hair. Come on, you must have seen her."

"I was just in the kitchen," she tells me. "I even went out into the yard to find a hose, so I'm pretty sure I'd have spotted someone. Besides, no-one's knocked on the door."

"I'm not making it up!"

"Okay, whatever, just -"

"Mom, I'm not!"

She sighs, and I can tell she doesn't entirely believe me. Then again, I probably sound nuts, so I don't really blame her. "Annie," she continues, "I get that your imagination is probably running overtime right now, but please don't come up with stuff like this. I would absolutely know if there had been a woman out there in the garden just now, and I'm sure she would have knocked. I mean, it's not impossible that one of the neighbors might make a trek out here to welcome us, but I don't think they'd just stand around in the garden and then leave without saying hello."

"There was someone out there," I reply, still watching the garden, convinced that the woman has to show up again. "Scott must have seen her. Ask him when he gets back."

"Annie..."

"I want my camera," I continue, turning to her. "Can you *please* find the boxes with my stuff in and bring them up? I want to get my digital camera out and have it ready. If that woman comes back, I'm gonna get a picture of her and then you'll have to believe me."

"I'm working through the boxes methodically."

"My boxes have my name on them."

"And I told you, I haven't found them yet."

"So they're lost?"

"They're down there somewhere," she continues, lifting the duvet and sliding the metal pan into the bed. "I'll be up in a few minutes to collect this, okay? Don't be embarrassed, just do your business." She heads to the door. "And I swear, I'll find something for you to read, even if it's just something from one of *my* boxes. I figured you might go stir crazy in this room, Annie, but I didn't think it'd happen on the first morning."

"I'm not crazy," I mutter, slipping the pan under myself. "There was a woman out there and she was -"

I let out a gasp as soon as I feel the cold metal against my skin.

"Where the hell did you keep this thing?" I hiss. "The fridge?"

As I do what I need to do in the pan, I turn and look back out the window. I know Mom thinks I'm going crazy up here in my room, like I'm some kind of wannabe *Rear Window* freak, but I know what I saw and I'm not quite at the stage yet where I'm going to start doubting my sanity. There was a woman in the garden, and something about her didn't seem right. Suddenly, being out here in this remote house feels even more unsafe than before. Good job I don't believe in ghosts.

At least, I *think* I don't believe in them.

CHAPTER FOUR

Seventy-one years ago

"THERE ARE A LOT more worms here," I tell Father as I scoop up some dirt in my right hand and watch the worms wriggling in the clumped soil. Some of them manage to squeeze between my fingers, which tickles, but I like it. "Why are there more in this part of the garden than everywhere else?"

"Mulch," he replies, digging more soil up as he works to create a new patch for vegetables.

That one word doesn't really answer my question, but I suppose it would be wrong of me to press the matter. I want Father to think that I'm learning. I turn my hand around in the sunlight, watching as the worms continue to wriggle, and then I smile as I let the handful of dirt fall to the ground. Looking down, I see the worms wriggling away from their crash, trying to find a way back underground. It's almost as if they're panicking. I can't help but smile.

"What's this for?" I ask, heading over to one of the trowels that's propped against an old tree trunk.

"It's a trowel," Father mutters.

"But it looks different to the others."

"It's for border work. You'll learn."

A moment later, I spot a hint of movement out of the corner of my eye. Turning, I see that Mr. Clement from the town is headed this way along the road that runs across our property. He rarely comes all the way out here, and when he does it usually means there's something important to discuss, so I can't help but feel a little concerned as I use my right hand to shield my eyes from the sun and watch him for a moment longer. He's walking fast, and the expression on his face strikes me as being a little unfriendly. Father won't like this; he never likes it when people come out to visit us from town, he prefers to be left alone.

"Father," I say, "Mr. Clement is here."

Taking a step back, I watch as Father drops his shovel and brushes his hands against his shirt, and then he adjusts his trousers and makes his way over to join the visitor. Just from the way he stomps across the grass, I can tell he's already annoyed.

"Go inside," he says sternly.

"But if -"

"Go inside."

Realizing that I must obey at once, I hurry to the back steps and then into the kitchen, although then I stop and wait, hoping to be able to hear the conversation that follows.

"Jonathan," Mr. Clement says, his tones sounding clipped and tense. As a member of the town council, he has no reason to be out here unless it's on official business, and if there's one thing I know Father hates more than any other, it's official business. I lean back around the doorway and watch as Mr. Clement reaches out to shake Father's hand. Father makes no move to reciprocate. "Fine day," Mr. Clement continues, forcing a smile that seems awfully hollow. "I see you've started work on your -"

"What do you want?" Father asks, interrupting him.

"Well, I was just in the area and -"

"What do you *want*, man?" Father asks again. "Can't you see I'm busy?"

"Of course." Reaching into his pocket, Mr. Clement slips out an envelope. "Truth be told, Jonathan, I'm here with a message for your wife. It's just that a letter came for her and it was being stored at the office, and I was hoping to pass it on to her at some point but she hasn't been into town in such a long time so I finally figured I should come out here and deliver it in person." He holds the envelope out, but Father doesn't take it. "I trust that Rebecca is in good health?" Mr. Clement adds, glancing toward the house.

I step back, to make sure I'm not seen.

"She's fine," Father replies. "There's no need for anyone to fuss."

I lean a little farther past the door-frame, so as to see them again.

"It's hardly fussing," Mr. Clement continues,

"it's just... Well, a few of us were talking and we realized it's been years since your wife was seen in town. Your daughter, too. Is Annie okay?"

"Annie's fine."

"I hear she hasn't been to school ever. Are you educating her yourself?"

"She can learn everything she needs from me."

"Even so -"

"Everything is quite alright out here," Father tells him, taking the letter. "I'll see to it that Rebecca receives this, and if there's any need to reply to whoever sent it, I'm sure she'll do so. I don't know why people bother writing letters, though. It's just another way of butting into everyone's business." He pauses. "Is there anything else you came out here for, Mr. Clement, or is your visit done with now?"

"Well..." Mr. Clement glances toward the house again, and I fear that he spots me briefly even though I step back out of sight. "We don't see much of any of your folk in town these days," he continues. "You must be doing very well with the land out here, not to need to come and fetch supplies."

"I know how to work my property," Father replies. "I don't need outside help."

"I'm sure you don't, it's just -"

"And part of that means getting on with work," Father adds, "and not wasting time on needless things. I'll make sure that my wife gets this letter, and I thank you for taking the trouble to come all the way out here. Other than that, Mr. Clement, I'm quite certain our business is concluded for today. I hope you'll enjoy the walk back to town."

I lean past the door-frame again, and I can't help smiling as I see the discomfort on Mr. Clement's face. Father is always so good at dealing with such people, and Mr. Clement is one of the worst of the people from town, all needly and officious.

"Well..." Mr. Clement pauses, but it's clear that he understands he's not welcome. "Of course, Mr. Garrett. It was good to see you again. Perhaps we shall have the pleasure of your custom in town some time soon?"

"Stranger things have happened," Father replies, taking up his shovel again and turning his back on Mr. Clement, so as to get back to work.

A moment later, Mr. Clement looks toward the house again, and this time we make eye contact briefly. I can't help giggling, and I can tell that my reaction has disquieted him. I pull back out of sight, and after a few seconds I realize I can hear him walking away. I stay hidden until I'm sure he's gone, and then I step out onto the porch and watch as Father continues to dig.

If I ever get married, I don't want a weakling like Mr. Clement. I want a real man, like Father.

CHAPTER FIVE

Today

"NO, SHE WON'T MIND at all," Mom says, as I hear multiple sets of footsteps coming up the stairs. "I think she'll be glad to meet new people."

Looking up from the old fashion magazine I've been reading, I realize that the visitors, whoever they are, are about to be brought up to meet me. I heard them knocking on the front door a few minutes ago, but I never imagined that Mom would actually let them see me when I'm in such a mess. Tossing the magazine aside, I quickly arrange the duvet before reaching over and sliding the window up, just to let some fresh air through.

I turn back to the door and begin to sit up, just as Mom appears with a smile and ushers a blonde woman and her equally blonde daughter into view. The visitors are both wearing such bright, garish clothes, I actually feel like I need sunglasses just to look at them.

"Annie," she says, "I want you to meet Harriet Roland and her daughter Tabitha. They live in that beautiful white house we passed on the way here, and they drove all the way over to welcome us to the neighborhood."

"Hi," I reply, forcing a smile. "Nice to meet you."

While Tabitha holds back a little shyly, her mother Harriet hurries into the room and reaches out to shake my hand. Suddenly there's an overpowering smell of over-applied cologne.

"My word," she says loudly, "what *happened* to you, you poor thing? You look like you've been in the wars!"

"Annie fell off her bike," Mom explains. "Well, more like she flew off and got launched over a railing. She ended up with two broken legs."

"How *awful*," Harriet continues, lifting the bottom of the duvet so she can see my plaster casts. She doesn't seem to care too much about personal boundaries. "Oh, how terrible." She turns to her daughter. "Tabitha, look at this poor girl! I've told you over and over to be careful on your bike, and now you can see why! Do you want to end up like this?" She waits for a reply. "Well, *do* you?"

"No," Tabitha says quietly. She seems painfully shy, although she might just be embarrassed by the way her mother came bowling into the room so noisily.

I know I would be.

"You must rest and get better," Harriet says,

turning to me. "Do you have a bell? You should have a bell, so you can get people to come up and bring you things. There's no harm in letting your family take care of you, you know. That's what they're there for. When I broke my ankle a few years ago, I made sure to press young Tabitha into service for a couple of weeks."

I look over at Tabitha and see that she looks so timid, it's almost as if she's about to shatter.

"Why don't you come downstairs for a cup of coffee?" Mom says, clearly sensing my discomfort. "Harriet, there's so much I don't know about the area, and we can try those brownies you brought over."

"What a marvelous idea," Harriet replies, heading to the doorway. "Tabitha, you must stay up here with Annie and get to know her. I'm sure you'll be friends in no time!"

Tabitha remains obediently just beyond the door as our mothers make their way to the stairs. Harriet is so loud, I swear I can make out every word she's saying, even once they get down into the kitchen. Meanwhile, Tabitha is simply loitering outside my room, avoiding eye contact and generally seeming as if she wants the ground to open and swallow her up. I mean, I'm not exactly the most sociable person in the world, but at least I can fake it from time to time.

"Do you want to come in?" I ask her finally, hoping she might perk up.

She glances at me quickly, before looking down at the floor again. She hesitates for a moment, before taking a couple of steps forward and then stopping at the foot of my bed.

"Do you want to... sit down?" I ask.

Again she seems hesitant, but after looking around for a moment, she takes a seat on the very end of the bed. For a moment, I find myself wondering if she'll literally do anything I tell her to do, although I figure it'd be rude to test that theory out. I can't help but notice that she's wearing pretty normal clothes, and I'm starting to think that I was getting carried away when I expected people around here to look totally backward. Once again, my imagination was running away with me.

"So you live nearby, huh?" I say after a period of excruciatingly awkward silence has passed.

She nods.

"In the white house, yeah?" I continue.

She nods again, and this time she lets out a faint murmur which I *think* might be "Yes."

"I saw that house when I arrived yesterday," I tell her, trying to strike a friendly tone. "It's, what, three or four miles away?"

She nods.

"And you're the closest neighbor?"

She nods.

"Well..." I pause, feeling as if this is the most one-sided conversation of my life. "I mean, it's good to know there are people out there somewhere," I continue. "Looking out the window, it's almost like this place is a million miles from anyone else, but I guess when I'm up on my feet again I'll be able to look around more." I pause again, keenly aware that Tabitha is looking down at her hands, which are resting in her lap. "So are there any cool places to check out?" I ask. "I have a bike, so when my legs are better, I can get about properly. There's a town not too far from here, isn't there? Dunceford?"

She nods.

"Is that a fun place to hang out?"

She pauses. "I guess," she whispers finally, which is something of an improvement.

"I used to live in New York," I tell her. "As you can imagine, coming out here is kind of a culture shock."

"I've never been to New York," she replies.

"But you've seen pictures, right?"

She pauses again, and then she nods.

"Well, the difference is crazy," I continue. "This time last week, I was living in one of the biggest cities on the planet. I had friends, I had places to go *all* the time, I had a life and I swear my phone never stopped ringing. Not that I was one of those cool people, you understand, but I definitely did more than sit in bed all day. Now look at me, I'm holed up in a manky room in a creaky old house, and there's nothing for miles around except... Well, I guess there's you, right?"

She nods.

"Sorry if that came out wrong," I add, feeling as if I'm talking too much. Then again, it's difficult when she only seems to answer with one word at a time. "So did you know the people who lived here before?" I continue, already starting to run out of things to say. Compared to this Tabitha girl, I'm positively loquacious.

She shakes her head.

"You didn't come to visit them?"

"They..." She pauses. "No-one lived here before

you."

"No-one? Okay, how long was it empty?"

"I think..." She glances at me briefly, before looking back down at her hands. "Seventy-one years, I think."

"Seventy-one years?" I stare at her for a moment. "This house was empty for *seventy-one years*?" I wait for her to reply. "What gives?"

"Well, there's..." She pauses again. "You know, there's the Barringer law about real estate in this county."

"The what?"

She flinches slightly, as if the mere effort of talking to me is making her skin crawl. "The Barringer law," she continues, her voice so low that I can barely hear a word she's saying. "The law says that anyone buying a house has to be told if a murder took place on the property at any point in the past seventy years."

"They do?"

"After seventy years," she continues hesitantly, "it no longer has to be mentioned."

"Huh." I pause. "So no-one bought the house until the seventy years were up?"

She shakes her head.

"So..." I pause again, suddenly realizing what this mean. "So you're saying that someone was murdered here?"

She nods.

"Who?" I ask, sitting up a little more. "Come on, you have to tell me. I had no idea about any of this!"

"There was a family," she replies. "Um, there's a

website with it on, maybe you should -"

"We've got no internet here yet," I tell her. "Please, just tell me what happened."

She flinches again. "I don't really... There was a family here, the Garretts I think their name was, apparently they didn't mix much with anyone from town and then the daughter..." She pauses, and yet again she glances briefly at me but seems to have to look away almost immediately. "The daughter died, or vanished, or something."

"Okay," I reply cautiously, "but... Who was murdered, then?"

"They found enough blood to know she was dead," Tabitha continues.

"But they didn't find her body?"

She shakes her head.

"So then what happened?"

"They convicted her parents. The parents got sent to the..." Her voice trails off.

"To the where?" I ask. "They got sent to jail for killing their own daughter?"

"Not jail," she replies, still looking down at her hands. "The electric chair."

I open my mouth to say something, but no words come out. Instead, all I can manage is to stare at her in shock for a moment. "Seriously?" I ask finally. "Are you sure you're not just trying to freak me out?"

"That's what I heard," she continues. "I mean, different... You know, there's different versions, but that's the basic one."

"And they *never* found the daughter's body?"

She shakes her head.

"Wow," I mutter, looking over at the window, "no wonder it took so long to sell the -"

Stopping suddenly, I think back to the woman I saw in the garden earlier. I lean over and peer out, but there's no-one there now. Still, a faint shiver runs through my body as I remember the way the woman was just standing there. I've never believed in ghosts, and I still don't, at least I don't think I do, but I can't help at least wondering who that woman was. Turning back to look at Tabitha, I see that she's started playing with her fingers, wriggling them in her lap like a nest of worms.

"Do you know a woman who wears white?" I ask cautiously. "Like, a white dress or gown, and she has black hair?"

She frowns. "Um... I don't think so."

"But there are other houses nearby, right? I mean, within a few miles?"

"We're the closest," she replies. "The Wayming family lives a little further off. Maybe ten miles."

"And is there a *Mrs.* Wayming there?"

She nods.

"Does she have black hair?"

"Um... Kind of dark brown."

I pause, thinking back to the sight of the woman, and after a moment I realize that her hair *might* have been dark brown after all. In the bright sunlight, it was kind of difficult to tell for certain.

"I guess it was her, then," I mutter, trying to keep from dwelling on the possibility. "Is she... I mean, is she kind of weird?"

"What kind of weird?"

"I don't know, like -"

"Tabitha!" Harriet calls up from the bottom of the stairs suddenly. "Don't forget your piano class at three! You'll have to come back another day to spend time with your new friend!"

Getting to her feet, Tabitha makes her way obediently to the door, as if she unthinkingly follows every order she's given by her mother.

"Feel free to drop by some time," I tell her, suddenly feeling as I really want to make a new friend. "I know I'm not very exciting right now, but when I'm out of this bed we could, I don't know, hang out or something?"

She mumbles a reply, but I can't quite make it out.

"What was her name?" I ask.

She stops on the landing and turns to me.

"The girl who was murdered here," I continue. "You said they were the Garretts, right? I was just wondering what the girl's first name was?"

She stares at me for a moment, and for the first time she doesn't avert her gaze at all.

"Annie," she says finally.

"I'm sorry?"

"Annie," she says again. "Her name was Annie."

I feel another shiver pass through my body. "*My* name is Annie," I point out cautiously.

She nods. "I know. Pretty weird, huh?"

With that, she turns and hurries away, and I hear the sound of the stairs creaking as she goes to join her mother. Harriet is saying goodbye to my mother – loudly – and already promising, or perhaps threatening would be the right word, to come and visit again soon. There's some talk of a barbecue when the weather improves, and of the two families getting together for dinner one night. As I listen to them talking, however, I can't help looking around my room and thinking about the story Tabitha just told me.

"Annie," I whisper, a little freaked out by the coincidence. "Well, that isn't creepy at all, is it?"

CHAPTER SIX

Seventy-one years ago

"LOOK AT IT!" FATHER shouts, pulling Mother over to my bedroom door. "Whose room is this?"

"It's Annie's," she stammers, with tears streaming down her face. "I know it's Annie's, I promise I won't -"

Before she can say another word, Father pushes her back against the opposite wall and reaches into his pocket, pulling out a small knife.

"Annie's room is for Annie," he continues, clearly annoyed. "She's old enough now that you shouldn't go into her room without being invited, is that understood?"

Mother nods.

"Is that understood?" Father shouts, stepping toward her.

"Yes!" she replies, holding her arms up to cover

her face.

"It's okay," I say calmly, standing next to my bed and watching as Father towers over her. "I think she realizes her mistake now, Father."

He looks down at her for a moment longer, before heading back to the door-frame and kneeling down. "I'm going to make damn sure she doesn't forget," he mutters as he starts carving something into the wood.

Stepping closer, I see that he's already inscribed the letter A.

"What are you doing?" I ask, but he doesn't answer.

Looking over at Mother, I see that she's shivering on the floor, as if fear has overtaken her. I know I should feel sorry, that I should have empathy for her, but instead I'm struck by the same feeling as always: I wish she'd smarten up and start acting in a way that makes Father not *have* to punish her. When I was a child, I learned pretty fast how to follow the rules in this house, but Mother just doesn't seem to have that ability. Sometimes I wonder if she's ever going to learn, or if she's going to have to be disciplined for the rest of her life. Is she stupid, or just stubborn?

"This is humiliating," Father mutters, still carving into the door-frame. "I shouldn't have to do this in my own home."

Turning to look at his work so far, I can't help but smile as I see that he's almost finished writing 'Annie's room'. His handwriting has always been loose and untidy, almost childlike, and using the knife isn't helping either; still, I feel a burst of pride in my chest as he finishes. He takes a piece of sandpaper from his pocket and uses it to file down the rough edges, and then he blows on the wood to get rid of any remaining shavings. Before I can thank him, he slips the knife away and then gets to his feet, before making his way over to Mother.

"No!" she shouts, covering her face with her hands again. "Please, I understand now!"

"Stop crying," he says firmly.

She nods, but the tears continue to flow

"Stop crying!" he roars, grabbing her by the collar and dragging her over to my door. He pulls her hands down and takes hold of the back of her head, holding her by the hair and forcing her face toward the door-frame. "Tell me what that says!"

She's sobbing, as if she might actually break down into hysterics.

"Tell me!" Father shouts.

"I can't!" she wails, adding something else that I can't quite make out.

"I think she's crying too much," I tell Father. "I don't think she can see properly for all her tears."

"Is that right?" He tilts her head back and stares down at her, and then he mutters something under his breath as he watches the tears flooding her eyes. "Are you going to stop crying, woman?"

She stares up at him. I don't think I've ever seen so many tears in someone's eyes before, they're positively overflowing.

"Are you going to stop?" he asks again.

"I don't think she can," I say after a moment.

"Look at her."

"Do you have a handkerchief, Annie?" he asks.

"I..." Looking around, I realize I don't. "No. I'm sorry."

Reaching into his pocket, Father pulls out the coarse sandpaper again. "I don't have one either," he explains, "so I guess this'll have to do."

"No!" Mother screams, trying to pull away.

"Get still!" he shouts, pushing her down and then rubbing the coarse sandpaper across her face, using it to wipe away her tears. She struggles some more, crying out, but she should know that resistance will only make him angrier. After all, he can't stop until she's learned her lesson, can he? He scrapes the sandpaper harder across her face, and although he tells her to keep her sobbing eyes open, she tries to squeeze them tight. Clearly annoyed, he starts rubbing the sandpaper in different directions, forcing her eyelids open and eliciting more cries of pain as finally beads of blood start running down the sides of her face. All the while, I can hear the sandpaper scraping through her skin.

"Father," I start to say, shocked by what I'm seeing. "I think -"

I pause, realizing that it's too late. She's angered him far too much, and now he's wiping her eyes furiously with the sandpaper, digging it deep into her eyes as she screams and tries in vain to push him away. Finally, after one more big, hard scrape, he stops drying her eyes and pushes her down onto the boards outside my door.

Shaken a little by what I just saw, I can't help

noticing that there's blood on the sandpaper's rough surface.

Down on the floor, Mother is sobbing as she clutches her face, and more blood is running onto her wrists and then down her arms. As she tries to sit up, I get a glimpse of the skin to one side of her eyes, and I can see scores of little scratches caused by the sandpaper. Still moaning with agony, Mother gets onto her knees and holds her hands a short way out, as if she's trying to look at something.

"I can't see!" she shouts, her voice filled with horror. "Help me! I can't see anything!"

***

"Won't be needing this, then," Father mutters as he drops the envelope onto the fire that's burning in the hearth. It's the same envelope Mr. Clement brought over this morning, but it's unopened, which I guess means he never gave it to Mother. "She can't read a letter if she can't see."

Turning back to Mother, I dip the cloth in a bowl of warm water and get back to work, dabbing at the cuts all around her eyes and the bridge of her nose. Even though Father's punishment was much harsher this time, I know deep down that Mother deserved it, and I also feel that Father wouldn't have gone so far if she hadn't provoked him. Her whole body is trembling, and her damaged eyes are open. I feel as if I can help with the cuts and scrapes *around* her eyes, but when it comes to the ones *on* the eyeballs... I shudder as I see the thin scratches that criss-cross her pupils. It's no wonder she's blind, and her eyes are watering a lot too, thanks to the small pieces that came off the sandpaper and got lodged in the white parts.

"It'll be okay," I tell her, even though that's a lie. The pale scratches on her pupils are too deep and large to ever heal, I'm sure of that.

She blinks, and more clear fluid runs down the side of her face. I'm not sure if she's crying, or if her damaged eyes are just leaking, or a little of both.

"Did you learn your lesson?" Father asks, making his way across the room and standing over her. He waits for a moment. "Well? Did you?"

She nods.

"Hold still," I tell her.

"Seeing as how I carved it into the wood," Father continues, "I don't see how being blind ought to stop you from reading what I wrote. It's Annie's room, and if you need reminding, just run your fingers across the wood in every frame in the house to check you don't go in there by accident. Do you understand?"

"Yes," she whimpers. "Do you think -"

She pauses.

"Do I think what?" he asks.

Her lips tremble, but no words come out.

"I think she wants to see a doctor," I tell Father. "She mentioned it earlier when you were out of the -"

Mother grabs my hand, squeezing it tight as if to keep me from saying too much.

"There's no doctor coming to *this* house," Father mutters, "and there's no-one from this house going to see a doctor either. I don't have the money to be paying for anything like that, so you'll just have to get by." He turns to walk away, before stopping and looking back down at Mother and then turning to me. "Do you think she's learned her lesson, Annie?"

"I..." Pausing, I stare into Mother's scratched eyes. "I think so," I say after a moment. "I mean... she certainly *should* have."

"I'm not convinced," he replies, "but we'll give her the benefit of the doubt." Reaching down, he puts a hand on my shoulder. "I'll be sleeping in your room tonight, Annie."

"Should I go in with Mother?" I ask.

"No, you can be in with me. Mother can sleep alone for a bit, until she's calmed down. Maybe that way she'll have time to think about what she's done. She can get that whimpering under control too, because there's no way in hell I'm putting up with it."

As he heads out of the room, I turn back to look at Mother's terrified face.

"I know this must be hard for you," I say after a moment, keeping my voice low so that Father doesn't overhear me offering her sympathy, "but I really hope that this time you learn how to -"

"Annie!" Father calls from the stairs.

"Coming!" Getting to my feet, I drop the cloth into the nearby bowl and quickly wipe my hands on the front of my apron. "You can find your own way up, can't you?" I add, heading to the door before glancing back at her. "Remember, if you can't see and you get a little confused, just feel on the door-frame and make sure it

doesn't say -" I pause. "Well, you know what I mean."
 "Annie!" Father calls again.
 "Coming!"

CHAPTER SEVEN

Today

"ANNIE, DO YOU WANT dessert?" Mom calls up from the bottom of the stairs.

"No thanks," I reply, "I'm full."

"Annie? Did you hear what I asked?"

"I'm full, thank you!" I shout back. "No dessert for me!"

"Annie?" Dad shouts. "Did I leave my phone in your room?"

I look around. "I don't think so!"

"Damn it," I hear him mutter.

"Annie!" Scott calls from one of the other rooms. "Did you pack the spare controller in one of your boxes?"

"I don't know!"

"Well it's not in mine!"

"Ask Mom!"

"Annie!" Dad shouts. "Are you sure my phone's not up there?"

"Yes, Dad," I reply with a sigh.

"Annie!" Scott calls out. "Annie, where are your boxes?"

"Annie!" Mom shouts from downstairs. "Do you want a drink?"

"No thank you," I tell her.

"Did you hear me?" she continues. "Annie?"

"Stop shouting that name!" I yell, momentarily overcome by frustration before quickly calming myself again. "Just... stop," I continue, looking around the room as I tell myself that I'm overreacting. I swear, all evening people have been shouting the name Annie every five goddamn seconds, and I'm starting to lose my mind.

Silence falls for a moment, and then I hear footsteps coming up the stairs. A few seconds later, Mom appears in the doorway with a frown.

"Annie, are you okay?"

"I'm fine," I reply, aware that I must seem flustered. I try sitting up in bed a little, before thinking better of it and settling back down. "Sorry, I just wish people would stop shouting Annie all the time, it's like..." I pause, trying to work out how I can explain the problem. It's not that I believe in ghosts, or that I believe that there could be anything in the house; at the same time, I just don't want to tempt fate by having people running around and shouting that name all over the place. "I just don't like the way everyone's shouting up to me," I add finally, figuring that even if I'm making myself sound grouchy, it's better than telling the truth and admitting that I'm worried. "Can you actually come up to my room when you want to ask me something, or better yet get me a new phone?"

Coming over to the bed, she takes her phone from her pocket and sets it down on my bedside table.

"You don't have to leave *your* phone with me," I tell her.

"It's late, I'm not going to use it tonight. Just hang onto it, and if anyone calls for me, take down a note. You can damn well earn your keep as my personal assistant." She pauses. "You're not finding this easy, are you?"

"I'm fine."

Smiling, she heads back to the door. "I'll tell your Dad and Scott to call you instead of shouting. I totally get how that must have been annoying."

"Thanks," I mutter, not wanting to let on quite how glad I am to have the phone. I know I'm being dumb, but I can't shake the feeling that something in this house isn't quite right. "By the way, does your phone have internet?"

"Sure does, but don't go crazy. The data charges are insane."

"I'll be quick," I reply, picking up the phone as she heads downstairs. I tap the screen to launch the web browser, and then I start searching for all the details Tabitha mentioned earlier. At first I don't manage to come up with any hits, so I try a few different search terms until finally I uncover a mention of Annie Garrett on a page about notable murders in the area. The phone takes a while to load the section, and there are only a couple of paragraphs:

> *Annie Garrett (1928 to 1944) disappeared shortly after her sixteenth birthday from her parents' remote home in the Albanack area of Caledonian Brunswick. A police investigation uncovered significant quantities of blood in the house, especially in Annie's bedroom, and a case containing her clothing – also bloodstained – was subsequently located in the forest near the family home. Suspicion immediately fell upon her parents, Jonathan and Rebecca Garrett, and the pair were arrested for Annie's murder in September 1944.*
>
> *The subsequent trial was controversial due to the lack of a body, but prosecutors argued that there was no doubt the girl had been killed. Jonathan and Rebecca Garrett, who with their daughter had lived an almost hermetic life away from other people, refused to testify or answer any questions, and in November 1944 they were found guilty of Annie's murder. The following year, they were both executed by electric chair, and their bodies were cremated in accordance with standard policy. To this day, the body of Annie Garrett has never been located, despite extensive searches on and near the family's property. No photos of Annie Garrett are known to have been taken.*

Scrolling down, I'm shocked to see a photo of our house, complete with forensic workers examining the garden. According to the caption, this photo dates from 1975, when the most recent attempt was made to locate Annie's body, thirty years after her death.

"Oh God," I whisper, feeling a shiver run through my chest, "we're living in an *actual* murder house."

I scroll further, hoping to see photos of Annie and her family, but there's nothing and I quickly find entries for other local murders instead. Closing the browser, I bring up Dad's number and tap the screen to call him, and then I wait until he picks up.

"Hey," he says, "is -"

"It's me," I tell him, "I'm using Mom's phone. So did you guys know what happened in this house seventy-something years ago?"

"Um..." He pauses, and I can hear him walking quickly. A moment later, I hear him on the stairs, and the call is cut as he comes into my room. "Hey, Annie, listen..."

"Did you *know*?" I ask again. "You did, didn't you!"

"It's complicated," he continues, shutting the door as he comes in and then sitting next to me. He keeps his voice noticeably low, as if he doesn't want anyone else to hear. "Annie, this house was a real bargain -"

"Because someone was murdered in it."

"Because of some dumb superstitions."

"Does Mom know?"

"Your mother doesn't *need* to know, she'd only... You know what she's like."

"I know what she's *like*?"

"Annie, please -"

"Do you know the murdered girl was also named Annie?"

"I -" He pauses, clearly shocked. "I'm sorry?"

"Her name was Annie Garrett," I continue. "She disappeared from this house in 1944, and she had the same name as me!"

"Well that doesn't mean anything," he replies, glancing at the door to make sure no-one can overhear us, before turning back to me. "Annie, listen, it's just a house, okay? There's nothing to be scared of."

"A girl went missing!"

"And I'm sure if her body was anywhere around," he continues, "it would have been found long before now. You have to be rational about this. Just because something bad happened here once, that doesn't mean we should turn around and run, okay? Hell, you stand in any spot on the planet, and I bet *someone* died there at some point in human history." He sighs. "I'm sorry about the name thing, that's an unfortunate coincidence, I had no idea the dead girl was called Annie as well." He looks toward the door. "Although I guess it explains the carving."

"What carving?" I ask.

"Oh..." He turns to me, and it's clear that although he'd rather not tell me, he knows he's let the cat out of the bag. "Your mother noticed it first. Someone scratched the words 'Annie's room' into the door-frame, that's all. We thought Scott must have done it, but I guess it's been here all along."

"This was her *room*?" I ask, my eyes widening with horror. "I'm in a murdered girl's bedroom?"

"No," he replies with a sigh, "you're in *your* bedroom, your *new* bedroom, and as soon as we get just a little bit sorted here, I promise this will be the first room we decorate." He waits for me to answer, as if he expects me to suddenly say that everything's fine. "Does that sound remotely like a good deal?"

"Did Mom tell you I saw someone in the garden?"

"I heard you had visitors earlier."

"No, I saw someone else." I turn and look out the window, although it's dark outside now. "There was a woman standing on the lawn. Mom didn't see her, but I swear she was there."

"Great," he sighs, "this is *exactly* why I didn't want anyone to know what had happened here. Your imaginations are all going to run wild, especially yours since you're cooped up in bed all day. You're not being rational, Annie -"

"So I should be rational and forget what I saw with my own two eyes? Does that even make sense?"

He stares at me for a moment. "Is this going to be a problem?" he asks finally.

"What do you mean?"

"I mean are you going to tell your mother about all of this? Are you going to dump all that worry on my shoulders?"

"I..." Pausing, I realize that he's desperate for me

to make some kind of deal. "Mom doesn't need to know," I admit reluctantly, "so long as nothing weird happens."

"Nothing will."

"But if something *does* -"

"Then we'll call the Ghostbusters and get it straightened out."

"You're not taking this seriously."

"Are you saying you think there's a ghost? Seriously?"

I open my mouth to reply, but I can't quite bring myself to come up with an answer. I mean, I believe in ghosts in movies and books, but in real life? That's quite a leap.

"It's just creepy," I tell him finally. "That's all."

"We're going to make this house ours," he replies, with a smile that I guess he thinks is supposed to be comforting. "Whatever happened here in the past, it's *staying* in the past. End of discussion. And whatever happens in the present day, please don't talk to your mother or your brother about this. Make sure to wipe the history of the browser on Mom's phone too, just in case." He gets to his feet. "I need to finish some stuff downstairs, but are you going to be okay on your own for a while?"

"Leave the door open," I tell him. "I don't want to be shut in here."

Once he's gone, I can't help bringing up the search again and trying again to find answers about the Garrett murder. I know deep down that there can't be such things as ghosts, but at the same time I'd like to see a photo of the family, just so I could be sure none of them looked like the woman I saw in the garden earlier. After another half hour, however, I have to admit defeat: the Garrett family appears to have been so reclusive, they didn't even leave any photos behind. I guess life was like that back then: you could live and die, and all you'd leave behind would be your name.

Later, after I've said goodnight to everyone, I start to nod off. It's strange how, from just sitting in bed all day, I can end up so tired. Just as I'm about to drift into a deeper sleep, however, I become vaguely aware of raised voices somewhere else in the house. They're not loud enough to wake me, but they keep rumbling along, preventing me from falling into a really deep sleep.

And then suddenly Mom screams.

CHAPTER EIGHT

Seventy-one years ago

FATHER IS SNORING NEXT to me, but I can't sleep.

The house is dark and quiet. I don't know what time it is, but as I stare at the open window I can see a blanket of stars filling the night sky and there's no hint of dawn yet, so I imagine it must be somewhere between midnight and five. In the morning, I'm to help Father in the garden again, but although I enjoy that kind of work, there's a part of me that wants the night to last forever. Everything feels so calm and peaceful, and I honestly can't imagine how life could ever be any better. I don't even want to sleep. I just want to be here, enjoying every precious second.

I hate sleepless nights, because whenever I can't sleep I end up thinking about the forest, and about the lake beyond the trees. I know I'm being foolish, and of course I've never mentioned any of this to Father or

Mother, but sometimes when I think about that lake in the moonlight, I can't help remembering the day I was out there a few years ago, swimming through the clear water. Even now, I remember how cool the water was against my body, and then I remember seeing that face, staring up at me with two dead eyes. Ever since then, things have been different. For one thing, Mother and I were much closer when I was a girl, but after the day at the lake, I've become much fonder of Father. Sometimes, I feel as if my way of seeing the world is all twisted.

Taking a deep breath, with Father still snoring next to me, I stare up at the dark ceiling and try to imagine how Mother must feel right now.

And then I hear it.

Somewhere in the house, beyond the closed door of my room, there's the faintest creaking sound, as if a foot was rested very gently against one of the loose boards.

I wait, hoping that I was wrong, but a moment later there's another creek, just slightly closer this time.

Not wanting to wake Father, I turn carefully and slowly until I'm looking over toward the closed door. With moonlight streaming through to the landing, I can just about make out a hint of light around the edges of the frame, and a moment later I see a shadow at the bottom, which can only mean one thing: having gone to bed a while ago, Mother is up and about. I listen for a moment, and then I spot another shadow, this time at the side of the door, near the handle. It takes a moment before I realize that Mother must be feeling for the scratched words in the wood.

Annie's room.

Once she's found those words, which she surely must have done by now, she should go away. Instead, I watch the door and realize that she's still out there, as if for some reason she's loitering on the landing. I want to call out and tell her to go back to her room, to tell her that Father and I are fine in here, but I'd still rather not wake Father so instead I simply watch the door, convinced that at any moment now she has to turn and walk away. After everything that has happened lately, I simply cannot believe that she would be so foolish as to not learn her lesson.

I wait.

Slowly, I start to hear a faint creaking sound.

The handle.

I watch as the door starts to inch open. I have no idea what Mother thinks she's doing right now, but she must have fully lost her mind if she thinks she can come in here. Glancing at Father, I can just about make out his sleeping face in the darkness, especially now that a little moonlight is coming through the opening door. Turning back, I see Mother's silhouette shuffling into the room, and I realize that with her damaged eyes she probably can't see me staring back at her. She's trying to be very quiet, and I watch with a sense of growing concern as she stops at the foot of the bed and sniffs the air for a moment. Shuffling forward, she starts to make her way around to Father's side, and then she stops and leans down again, sniffing as if to make sure that it's him. She clearly has no idea that I'm awake.

Now that she's closer, I can hear the faintest of

sobs coming from her silhouette.

Reaching down, she fumbles with something near her waist, and that's when I realize that she's holding one of the shovels from the garden. For a moment, I truly can't imagine what she's doing, but then slowly, with tremblings hands, she starts to raise the shovel, almost as if she's going to strike down with it against the bed. The idea is so monstrous, so horrifying, that at first I can't believe it's true, until she holds the shovel high above her head and tilts the tip slightly, as if to aim directly at Father. All the while, her body is trembling.

And then she strikes.

"No!" I shout, launching myself toward her and slamming into her chest, sending her crashing back against the wall. I feel the edge of the shovel's head cutting against my chin, but there's no time to deal with that now. Instead, I focus on pushing Mother down to the floor and placing a hand over her mouth, trying to quieten her shrieks. I climb on top of her, using my knees to press into her ribs and belly, and I lean closer as she struggles to get free.

"What the hell is going on in here?" Father shouts from the bed.

"I've got her!" I shout back, forcing Mother down more firmly this time. Out of breath and with my heart pounding faster than I've ever known before, I feel for a moment as if I want to hit Mother, to make her pay for her gross idiocy. Turning, I see that her hands are reaching out, trying desperately to find the shovel. I kick the damn thing away, sending it clattering under the bed so she can't get to it.

"What's she doing in here?" Father asks, stepping off the bed and towering over us both.

"I don't know," I stammer, as she continues to try fighting me off. "I just heard he come in and then -"

Reaching down, Father pulls the shovel out from under the bed, banging it against the frame in the process, and then he holds it up.

"Father," I say after a moment, worried that he's coming to the same conclusion I already reached, "please, don't think the worst. I'm sure she -"

"Get aside, Annie," he says firmly.

"Father -"

"Get aside."

I pause, and he grabs me by the collar, pulling me back against the bed as he steps over Mother. She's still struggling to get up, but she freezes as soon as father presses the head of the shovel against her belly and then puts his right foot on the edge, ready to drive it down into her guts as if he were digging in the garden.

"No!" she shouts, her trembling hands reaching down toward the shovel. She tries to push it away, holding onto the rusty edges, but Father just presses down harder with his boot until she lets out a cry of pain.

"What did you intend to do in this room tonight?" Father bellows. "Tell me the truth, or I swear I'll dig through you like you're a knot of weeds!"

"Stop!" she screams, so loud that I briefly worry the neighbors might hear five miles away. "For the love of God, don't hurt me! Please don't hurt me! Please, please..." Her shaking fingers are still holding the sides of the shovel, but she can surely not hope to force it away.

"Or what?" he asks, with his foot still resting on the shovel's head. "You came in here meaning to hurt me, didn't you?"

"No!" she shouts. "I swear on all that's holy, I just got the wrong room!"

Father turns to me. "What was she doing when she came in?"

"She..." Staring down at Mother, I see the terror in her scratched eyes and I realize that I have power over her. I could lie to Father, he'd most likely believe me, but at the same time I know that lying is a sin. I've been taught that all my life. "She felt the door-frame," I say after a moment. "I could see her shadow, I could tell she was -"

"No!" Mother shouts. "Don't listen to her!"

"I saw her shadow," I repeat, turning to Father. "She was out there for a little while, making sure which room she was at. Then she opened the door quietly and carefully, so as not to wake us up." I turn back to Mother, and I can see pure fear in her damaged eyes. At the same time, she must know I can't be sinful. "You know it's true," I tell her. "I'm not to lie, am I?"

"Please," she whimpers, clutching the head of the shovel as it continues to push down against her belly. Breaking into a series of sobs, she says a few other things that are inaudible, before tilting her head back and letting out a wail of pain. "Do it!" she shouts. "End it all now! Kill me and bury me in the garden! I don't want to live like this anymore! My eyes hurt so much!"

I swallow hard, waiting to see whether Father will do what she wants. For a moment, it seems as if he truly might dig down into her until the shovel's metal tip reaches through to the floorboards, severing her body and ending her life. I think he might truly be considering that option, but finally he moves his foot away and pulls the shovel back, tossing it onto the bed.

"Just do it," Mother whimpers, clutching her belly. "Lord have mercy on my soul!"

"She meant to kill you," I tell Father. "Of that, I have no doubt."

"Nor do I," he says firmly. "Annie, go make the basement ready."

"The basement?" I pause, surprised by his command. "Ready for what?"

"Just clear the far end of any tools, anything she might be able to use. I want it bare." He turns to me. "Go!" he barks.

Stumbling back, I turn and hurry to the door, ignoring Mother's continued sobs. I must confess that as I make my way downstairs, I feel a little shocked, and by the time I get to the basement door and pull the bolt across I'm almost trembling with fear. Not just fear, though. Excitement too, and anticipation. I pull the door open and take a candle from the shelf, lighting it so as to be able to see my way. As I start to make my way down the steps, however, I hear Mother crying out from upstairs, and then I hear a bump, almost...

Was that the shovel striking the floorboards? Did Father change his mind and end her life?

I pause for a moment. A few seconds later, I

realize I can still hear Mother sobbing, and I can hear Father stomping about up there.

Heading into the basement, I set the candle down and then get to work, hurriedly pulling the tables from the far end and setting them near the foot of the steps. I'm not certain what Father intends to do down here, but I have an idea, and it's clear that he wants to ensure Mother can't get hold of anything she might use as a tool, either to hurt one of us or to cause harm to her own self. Once I've cleared the far end, I take another look around to make sure that there's absolutely nothing she might find useful, and then I head toward the steps, only to hear the sound of Mother struggling at the top. Seconds later, I see a dark shape being shoved through the door and I step back just in time to avoid being struck as Mother is sent rattling down the steps. She lands hard in a crumpled heap at my feet.

Stepping back, I gasp as I see that her right ankle is broken and twisted back, most likely from the fall. She's sobbing more than ever.

Father makes his way down, stomping so hard on each of the creaking old steps, I'm worried he might break them.

"You can go upstairs now, Annie," he tells me, untwisting a section of rope in his hands. "I can handle this. Go back to bed. You need to sleep."

"What are you going to do?" I ask, watching as he grabs Mother's collar and starts pulling her across to the basement's far side.

"Something I should have done a long time ago," he replies.

"But what?"

"It's none of your concern."

"But is she -"

"Get out!" he shouts, turning and pushing me back toward the steps. "Don't make me tell you again, girl!"

"I'm sorry," I reply, hurrying up the steps until I reach the door, at which point I stop and look back down. I can hear Mother still sobbing, and in the candle's low light I can just about make out Father still holding the rope as he heads over to her. She's on the floor, curled up like a little dead baby, as Father stops and reaches down to her. Realizing that it's not my place to interfere, I head up and push the door shut, before making my way across the kitchen.

I can hear Mother crying out in the basement below. Whatever Father's doing to her, I hope that this time, *finally*, she might actually learn to mend her ways.

CHAPTER NINE

Today

"WHAT'S WRONG?" I SHOUT, trying once again to make them hear me as I sit up in bed. "Mom? Dad? Can someone *please* talk to me?"

I can hear them out there on the landing. It's two in the morning and Mom sounds like she's freaking out, and I can tell Dad's trying to calm her. Just a few seconds earlier, Mom's scream rang through the house, and now I'm waiting for one of them to come in and tell me what the hell is going on. A moment later, Scott steps into the doorway wearing his pajamas, and he stares toward Mom and Dad's room before turning to me. From the look in his eyes, I can tell he's worried.

"What's wrong?" I ask. "Is Mom okay?"

He shrugs.

"I want to know what's happening!" I shout.

"Go back to bed!" Dad says firmly from further

along the landing. "Both of you!"

"I'm already *in* bed," I point out, as my brother – who's clearly a little freaked out – steps into my room. "Scott," I continue, "can you *please* tell me what's going on? I can't exactly get out of bed to go look myself!"

"I think Mom had a bad dream or something," he replies, although the usual confidence is gone from his voice and he seems significantly more subdued. "I heard her... I don't know, she was whispering in their room, I could hear her through the wall, and then she started screaming." He peers back out onto the landing. "Dad's got her back into the room now. He'll make sure everything's okay."

"Is she okay?" I ask, starting to feel increasingly frustrated by the fact that all I can see beyond my room is a couple of square foot on the landing. "Scott, just tell me what the hell is going on."

"Something really freaked her out," he continues. "I don't know, Dad seems to have it under control. I've never seen her life that before, it's like she was really scared." He looks along the landing for a moment longer, before turning to me. "What would make Mom scream like that?"

"I don't know," I reply, my heart pounding in my chest. "I've never heard her act like this before. It's almost like -"

Suddenly I hear footsteps coming closer to the door, and a moment later Dad comes into view.

"Bed," he says firmly. "Both of you. Now."

***

"Lift your arm," Mom says the following morning, as she continues to give me my latest sponge bath. "Higher, Annie. Come on, be cooperative."

"I *am*," I reply, holding my left arm up as high as I can manage. "I'm being *very* cooperative. *You're* the one who isn't cooperating, you won't tell me what happened last night."

"I *did* tell you, it was -"

"Nothing, sure." I flinch as she wipes under my arm with cold soapy water. For the first time, she hasn't remembered to heat the water for my bath. "I just don't believe you," I continue. "I heard the way you were crying out, something obviously got to you."

"I had a nightmare."

"Must've been a hell of a nightmare. What was it about?"

"I don't remember."

I raise a skeptical eyebrow. "Was it about this house?"

She glances at me for a moment, before shaking her head. "No, of course not. What makes you ask that?"

"It's a reasonable assumption," I continue. "We've only been here for a few nights now, I can imagine it's starting to get to you. The place *is* kind of creepy."

"It's natural for a new house to seem a little off," she replies. "I'm not going to go overreacting just because a few things have fallen over and a couple of bumps have woken me in the middle of the night."

"Things falling over?" I ask with a frown.

"Bumps in the night?"

"It's nothing."

"If one more person says that to me..." I wait for her to continue, but I think she's hoping I'll just drop the subject. "Has weird stuff been happening to you?"

She dips the sponge in water again, before starting to clean my left arm. "I'd rather not talk about it," she says eventually. "Nothing happened, it's just a bunch coincidences."

"Yeah, like my name being -" I catch myself just in time, remembering that Dad told me not to mention the Garrett family murder to Mom. I'm not entirely comfortable with the idea of keeping things from her, but at the same time I know this probably isn't the right moment to bring up something so momentously creepy. "What kind of coincidences?" I ask.

"Silly ones that don't mean anything."

"Like?"

She sighs. "Like... Just doors..." She pauses, followed by another sigh. "It doesn't matter."

"Tell me," I reply, seeing the hint of concern in her eyes. "I've heard a few odd bumps over the past few days, mostly downstairs." I wait for her to say something. "I *know* you," I continue. "I know when you're worried, and I heard you last night. That was more than a nightmare. People don't really wake up screaming in the night from a bad dream, not in the real world, not the way *you* screamed."

She pauses, and I can tell she's on the verge of opening up.

"Please, Mom," I continue. "You know you can

talk to me, right?"

"Don't tell your father I mentioned this," she replies, lowering her voice, "but I just... I woke up in the middle of the night and for a moment I thought I saw someone standing next to the bed." She sighs, as if she's embarrassed to admit such a thing but maybe also a little relieved. "It was only for a second, I was looking up and I saw this figure right there, just inches away from me, looking down and... It was such a clear image, even now I can see it perfectly, and I froze."

"So it was a dream, then," I reply. "It must have been."

She stares at me, and I can tell she isn't convinced.

"Dreams can be pretty convincing," I point out. "Sometimes they can seem like they're really happening."

She nods.

"But?" I continue. "What else happened, Mom?"

"I could feel it," she replies. "I can't even explain that part, but I could feel a presence, and I just stared up at the shape and I felt this real anger being directed toward me, as if... It was dripping, too. That's the craziest part, the figure was dripping, like its clothes were soaking wet, and then after your father had calmed me down, I went back and checked the floor next to the bed and..."

I wait for her to continue.

"And what?" I ask, even though I think I already know what she's going to say.

She shakes her head.

"Were there drips on the floor?"

"Your father thinks there must have been a leak in the ceiling," she replies cautiously.

"Was it raining last night?" I ask.

She shakes her head again.

"And is there a hole in the ceiling?"

"No."

"So -"

"He thinks the drips caused me to have the dream," she explains. "He's going to go up and check the ceiling properly, make sure it's fixed." She pauses, as if she's reliving the moment, and then suddenly a relieved smile crosses her face, mixed with a little embarrassment. "It was just a night terror," she says, as if she's trying to convince herself as much as me. "You see how easy it is to get spooked? I've been so busy warning you not to let your imagination go crazy, I forgot to keep from doing it myself."

"But if -"

"I'll just grab some fresh water," she adds, getting to her feet and heading to the door, "and then we can watch a movie, if you like? I feel so bad, thinking about you being up here alone and -" Stopping in the doorway, she looks out to the landing for a moment, almost as if she's nervous. She glances both ways, before forcing another smile and stepping out. "Everyone else is out," she continues, clearly trying to hide the fact that she feels scared. "We'll sit in here together. I'll be back in a few minutes, okay?"

As she heads to the bathroom, I can't shake a sense of concern. My mother, my usually rational and level-headed mother, seems to have changed in just half a day; she's obviously shaken now and trying to hold herself together, and I'm pretty damn sure that despite everything she just told me about her experiences in the night, there's a lot more that she kept back for fear of sounding crazy. She's not the kind of person who'd ever want to cause problems for other people, so most likely she's internalizing her fears, but I have no doubt that she's scared.

I still don't really believe in ghosts, but the fact that my mother's scared of something in the house? *That* scares me.

CHAPTER TEN

Seventy-one years ago

"I MADE THE POTATOES a different way," I tell Father as I put his plate in front of him. "I hope you like them."

Picking up his fork, he nudges the potatoes, smearing them through the gravy. He seems to be making patterns; sometimes I wonder what really goes on in Father's head, and I'm quite certain that he thinks a lot more than he lets on. Men like Father – quiet, hard-working men who don't air their thoughts so much – are easily written off as simple, but I happen to believe that in many cases they're actually the most contemplative people of all. There are definitely currents in Father's moods, and I understand why he never opens up to Mother. Perhaps, however, he'll learn over time that he can talk to me a little more. I'd like that.

"I used goose fat," I explain, starting to worry

that he won't like the change. "I thought... Well, I know how much you like goose fat on lamb, so I thought it might work equally well on the potatoes."

I watch as he cuts off a slice and slips it into his mouth.

"If you don't like it," I continue, "I can go back to doing them how Mother used to."

He chews for longer than usual, before swallowing.

"They're fine," he mutters, as he starts cutting off a section of meat. "You're a good cook, Annie. That's one of the few things I don't mind you learning from your mother. You're actually better than her."

I can't help but smile with pride.

Hearing a faint bump from beneath the floor, I look down and find myself wondering what, exactly, Mother is doing down there. It has been two days now since Father dragged her down, and she hasn't been back up since. Father hasn't explicitly told me that I'm not to check on her, but I feel I need his permission and I'd rather not ask. He'll tell me when he's ready. I know she's still alive, because I can hear her sometimes, but I haven't yet summoned the courage to ask Father about the situation directly. I feel it's his job to discipline her, not mine, and I should be patient. For the past couple of nights, I've heard her screams from down there, so I assume he's getting the job done just fine.

Right now, however, I can hear a scratching sound. It's almost as if she's reaching up and trying to claw her way out through the ceiling. A moment later I hear a faint snap beneath my feet. Did one of her fingernails just break off?

"Don't go worrying about her," Father says after a moment. "Don't think about it."

Turning to him, I realize my concern must have been obvious.

"Sorry," I reply, heading to the stove to fetch my own food.

"Some people never learn properly," he continues. "It's a curse."

"How..." I pause. "How long will she be down there?"

"How *long*?" He lets out a loud sniff, which is his way of laughing. "Well, I sure as hell don't have any plans to let her up again today, so I think she'll be waiting a good long time." He sniffs again. "We'll see."

"Of course," I reply, setting the food on my plate before heading over and taking a seat opposite him. I don't have much appetite, but at the same time I know that Father thinks family meal times are very important. He's a real family man, and I know he appreciates the time we spend together, even if he doesn't say as much. As I settle and prepare to eat, however, I can tell that he's troubled this evening, to the point that he seems to have lost his appetite.

I wait, hoping his mood will recover.

"If you don't like the food," I say finally, "I can -"

"It's not the food."

"Well..." Pausing, I try to work out what I've done wrong. "Is it... If I've displeased you in any way, Father, I would rather know at once, so I can remedy my behavior. Mother never really taught me very much about managing the house, I suppose that's another of her failings but I'm sure I can learn if you just..."

My voice trails off as I watch him close his eyes. Whatever's wrong, he's clearly very troubled indeed.

"What is it?" I ask, getting to my feet and making my way around the table. Stopping behind Father, I put my hands on his shoulders, and immediately I can feel the tension. His muscles are rigid, especially on the right side, and I can't help wondering whether all his recent exertions have left him injured. I'm sure there are plenty of simple cures for such things, but I wouldn't know where to start. If only Mother had taught me properly, I'd be better placed to take over her duties. Still, I saw her massaging his neck and shoulders once or twice, so I start trying to do the same.

"Go back to your seat," he says after a moment, rubbing his face as if he's tired.

"I know you didn't sleep well last night," I tell him, keeping my hands on his shoulders. I'll go to my seat if he tells me again, but for now I would prefer to stay close, to maybe find a way to help him. "Was that my fault? Did I move too much during the night and keep you awake?"

"It wasn't that."

"If you wish," I continue, "you could strap me down so that I -"

"It wasn't you," he says again, with just a hint of irritation in his voice. Reaching up, he pushes my hands off his shoulders. "Quit doing that, girl, and quit talking so much. You're giving me a headache."

"I'm sorry," I tell him. "I'm just... Mother really should have taught me what to do."

"I will go back to sleeping in the other room tonight," he replies. "I think it might be best."

"But why?" I ask, shocked by the idea. In just a few nights, I have become accustomed to having Father next to me during the night. "Father, if I'm doing something wrong -"

"You're not," he replies, "I just..."

He sighs.

"Let me show you that I can be better," I tell him, looking down at the back of his head. "Let me prove myself to you."

"Annie -"

"You *should* be in my room," I continue, trying not to sound too panic-stricken as I try to think of a solution. "People should sleep near each other, it's only right. I mean, for warmth if nothing else, but also for safety. Or... I could be in *your* room, I suppose."

"Your room is for you."

"It's for both of us," I point out. "If you wish, we could add your name to the door and -"

"I'm going to bed," he says suddenly, getting to his feet and pushing past me. Stopping in the doorway, he glances back at me with tired, labored eyes. "I usually take a plate down to your mother after dinner, but tonight I'm too... You'll have to do it. No cutlery, she's not allowed that. God forbid that woman gets hold of a fork in her current state. Tell her I'll be down to talk to her in the morning. I think it's time we start thinking about bringing her back up."

"But you said -"

"I think she's most likely learned her lesson by now."

"You can't be sure of that," I reply, feeling for some reason a hint of concern at the thought of Mother returning. The truth is, I've rather liked having her out of the way, and the idea of bringing her back up feels like a defeat. "Don't rush things, Father."

"Take her some food," he mutters, turning and heading out into the hallway and then up the stairs.

Making my way to the door, I stop and listen to his heavy footsteps. When he gets to the landing, he seems to hesitate for a moment, as if he's not sure which room to enter and which bed to sleep in, and I hold my breath for a few seconds until I hear the boards creak and the sound of my door opening. With a faint smile, I realize that he's entered my room after all, which is how things should be. I can handle anything down here, truly I can, so long as I know that I shall be able to sleep alongside him tonight.

Looking down at the kitchen floor, I realize that there's one more task I must complete before I go up to join Father.

***

The metal plate clangs unpleasantly as I set it down on the concrete floor. With just the light of a candle to help me see, I look across the dark basement toward the shadows at the far end, and I wait for Mother to show herself. As the seconds pass, however, I start to realize that the room feels perfectly silent and still, almost as if...

I hold my breath.

Almost as if Mother is dead.

A moment later, I hear the faintest of scraping sounds, and I breathe again. Mother is alive, albeit scared and apparently unwilling to come any closer. I know Father has tied her with ropes, and I know those ropes are attached to the old ironing stock in the corner which means she can't possibly drag herself free, but from the mess of sour gravy on the floor I can tell that Mother must be able to at least reach the middle of the room. There's really no reason for her to hold back. It's almost as if she's scared of me, but that's a ridiculous idea.

"Come on," I say with a smile, tapping the side of the plate with a fingertip. "You must eat."

I wait.

After a few seconds, I realize I can hear her breathing. From the sound of it, she seems to have almost become some kind of animal.

I force my smile to remain hidden, but I can't deny a sense of relief. After all, if Mother has become such a brute so quickly, how can Father ever think to bring her back upstairs? It's amazing how quickly someone can lose their civilized manners, although perhaps Mother's manners were never deeply-set to begin with. She was from lowly, common stock when Father met her, and I've always wondered why he took pity on her and married her when they were both so young. I suppose he just wanted to get the whole thing over and done with, so he took the first wife he could find. He could most certainly have done better if he'd waited.

"You must come closer," I tell her. "I can't just leave the plate here. Perhaps that's how Father does things, but I want to see your face. I also want you to thank me, because -"

Stopping suddenly, I think back to the moment when Father used the sandpaper on her eyes.

"But you're blind, aren't you?" I continue, having not remembered that fact previously. For a moment, I almost feel sorry for her. "Well, no excuse, you must come toward the sound of my voice if you want to eat."

I wait.

Silence.

"Come!" I say firmly, deciding to try a different approach. "Right now, Mother! Come!"

I wait again, and this time there's a faint shuffling sound. Peering into the darkness, I start to make out the faintest of shapes, and then an arm moves into the light, dirty and almost yellow with bruises. A moment later, as if by shifting her position she has disturbed the air in the basement, I become aware of the most horrible smell, which I suppose must come from the fact that Mother has been relieving herself down here. Disgusted by the stench, I want to turn and go upstairs immediately, but I force myself to stay in place as she crawls a little further forward. Finally I see her face and, as she comes closer, the flickering candlelight picks out her damaged eyes perfectly, even marking the scratches that run across her pupils. Those scratches seem almost ghostly white now.

"Just a little further," I tell her. "This isn't so bad, is it? What are you afraid of?"

She stops, looking in my direction but not directly at me.

"You mustn't worry about Father," I continue. "I'm doing a fine job of looking after him, and the house too. You really should have taught me better in case this day came, but what's done is done and I'm learning quickly. In fact, I'd go so far as to say that I'm performing remarkably well, it's almost as if I was born for this role." I pause, watching her wretched face, and after a moment I realize with a flash of pride that she really *is* scared to come closer. My own mother fears me. "Do you think I intend to beat you?" I ask with a smile. "It's Father's place to punish you, not mine. Mother, really, don't be so foolish. Come closer, you must know that I won't hurt you."

I wait.

"Come," I continue. "If you want to eat, you have no choice. Or shall I take the plate back up?"

After a moment, she crawls a little further forward. Her clothes are torn and stained, with her pretty white dress having been ripped in several places, and her long black hair is hanging down in dirty, straggly knots. As she gets closer to the plate and reaches out with a trembling hand, she truly resembles a mangy dog far more than she resembles a civilized woman.

"There," I say with a grin, which I suppose she cannot see, "isn't that better?"

Her hand fumbles for the plate, feeling its edges as if she's searching for cutlery, before finally she scoops some potato into her palm and moves it to her lips. I can't help but wince as I watch her licking the food from her dirty skin, but at the same time I know full well that she brought this on herself. She simply never learned how to keep Father from getting angry.

After a moment she edges closer still, as if her fear has begun to dissipate. She focuses on eating, while I watch her bare shoulder. Looking down at my right hand, I find myself contemplating the damage that I could cause if I just sliced her flesh with one of my nails. I know I told her that it's Father who doles out the punishments, but still, I should at least like to know how it feels to wield that power, and besides, I liked the idea that Mother was starting to fear me and suddenly I don't want that fear to fade. She should see Father and I as her clear superiors, especially if there's any chance of her coming up to the main part of the house again. Finally, I reach out and move a fingertip toward the skin of her shoulder, and I wait until she's almost finished eating before I quickly slice my nail against her.

She lets out a yipped cry and recoils, scurrying back into the shadows.

A broad smile crosses my face, and when I look at my finger I see a hint of blood under the nail. I know it's wrong of me to take on one of Father's tasks, but I truly can't deny that it feels good to experience a sliver of his power. It's almost as if I'm an extension of him.

Half an hour later, once I've gone back to the kitchen and washed the dishes, I'm finally ready to go to bed. I notice some drips on the kitchen floor, but when I look at the ceiling I'm unable to see any kind of hole. Getting onto my hands and knees, I wipe the drips up, keen to ensure that the house is tidy and clean. This, after all, is honest work. Finally, a little before midnight, I'm done, and I feel a sense of great satisfaction before heading upstairs.

When I get to the landing, I open the door to my room and see Father sleeping in the bed. I feel as if he has doubts still, and I have to find a way to ease those doubts so that Mother isn't rehabilitated and brought back up. I suppose it will just take time. Besides, Mother is such a mess now, it's clear she can never resume her old position. Smiling, I step into the room and push the door shut.

CHAPTER ELEVEN

Today

"YOU LOOK STUPID," SCOTT says, sitting on a chair in the corner of my room and watching as I get ready to stand. "You know that, right? You look really, really -"

"Thanks for the pep talk," I reply, wedging the crutches in my armpits. "You're a real confidence-booster, you know that? You should think about a career in motivational -"

Feeling a pinch of pain in my right knee, I let out a gasp.

"Loser," Scott mutters.

I've spent all day psyching myself up to try the crutches, but now that the moment is here I can't help feeling a little worried. What if I can't do this? I've been in bed for three days now and I swear I'm going to go stir crazy if I don't manage to get out of this goddamn room, but at the same time my plaster-encased legs are already starting to hurt just from the effort of swinging them over the bed's side, and now even the thought of lifting myself up with the crutches and trying to reach the door... Well, let's just say that in my current state, even a simple task feels like way too much.

"Are you going to do this or not?" Scott asks. "And why do *I* have to be here?"

"I'm going to do it," I mutter, adjusting the crutches, "and you don't *have* to be here, I just don't want Mom and Dad to know I'm trying this and I figured you could help."

I take another moment to compose myself, before counting down from three in my head and finally starting to haul myself up. The effort is way, way more than I expected, and I feel as if I'm about to collapse as I slowly raise myself on the tottering crutches. Holding my breath, I eventually let out a gasp as I set just a little weight on my less-damaged-of-the-two right leg, hoping against hope that I might be able to at the very least hobble about. Damn it, I knew this would be hard, but I never expected it to be *this* bad.

"I think people with crutches need to have one good leg," Scott points out. "I don't think this is going to work."

"Quiet!" I hiss, steadying myself. The pain in my legs – both of them – is way more than I'm willing to let on right now. "I'm going to try to make it to the door."

"If you fall over and hurt yourself, it's not my fault."

Ignoring him, I try to turn toward the door,

before realizing that even this simple movement feels like a Herculean task. I stop and try to consider alternatives for a moment, but finally I figure that I have to somehow scooch the crutches an inch or two at a time. To be honest, I'm already realizing that this whole experiment is a mistake, and if Scott wasn't watching and commenting on the whole thing, I'd be giving up right about now. Then again, I figure I just need to have a little more confidence.

"Mom and Dad are being weird," he says after a moment.

"Sounds about right."

"I mean *weird*," he continues with a frown. "I don't like it."

Seeing the sense of concern in his eyes, I realize my brother is doing something he's never done before: he's actually opening up to me about his feelings. Glad of the chance to just rest on the crutches and delay the attempt to turn, I wait for him to continue, but he seems almost nervous. First Mom started acting out of character, and now apparently it's Scott's turn.

"Go on," I say finally. "Details."

He shrugs.

"Give me an example," I add.

"Mom was in the basement after lunch," he continues, "and when I went down to see what she was doing, she shooed me out like a dog. She was acting like she had something down there she didn't want me to see."

"It's your birthday in two months," I reply. "Maybe she's just really organized this year."

"And then Dad got back from the store and when he realized she was down there, he got, like, really mad. Really, *really* mad."

"That doesn't sound like Dad," I point out. "I didn't hear anything from up here."

"I heard them from the kitchen," he replies. "Dad was telling her off down there, and then it sounded like..." He pauses. "It sounded like he was pushing her up the stairs really hard. Now she's got this bruise on her arm."

I stare at him for a moment.

"Dad wouldn't *hurt* Mom, would he?" he asks finally, and it's clear that he's worried. Either that, or he's gotten a lot better at trolling me since his last pathetic attempt.

"Dad would *never* hurt Mom," I reply, trying not to dwell too much on such a crazy idea. "I think you must've got the wrong end of the stick somehow. I'm sure Dad wasn't mad at her, and there are a million ways someone could get a bruise on their arm." I wait for him to say something, but he seems to have sunk into his own thoughts. One thing's certain: he's not making any of this up, he's genuinely worried. "What's in the basement, anyway?"

He shrugs again.

"You haven't been down there?" I ask. "Seriously? I thought you were, like, exploring the whole house?"

"Dad keeps it locked."

"So where's the key?"

"There's a key to the lock, and there's also a

padlock, and that needs a key too. I don't know where either of them are, and he told me not to go down there."

"He did?" Pausing, I can't help thinking that there have to be a few elements missing in this story. After all, the behavior Scott's describing sounds nothing like Dad at all. The last thing I need is for all three of my closest family members to starting acting out of character. "I really don't think I'm up to getting all the way to the basement on these crutches," I tell him, "but why don't you just find the keys when Mom and Dad are out, and then you can look?"

"Dad told Mom he's keeping the keys on him," he replies. "He told her he doesn't trust her anymore."

"He said those exact words?"

He nods.

"Well..." Although I want to dismiss everything he's saying, I can see the genuine fear in his eyes, and even though I don't want to admit it, I really don't think my little brother is capable of pulling off such a convincing lie. He *is*, however, capable of putting two and two together and coming up with completely the wrong answer.

"I heard scratches, too," he continues.

"Scratches?"

"Like something scratching under the kitchen floor last night. Mom and Dad were in the front room, so I know it wasn't them."

"It must have been a mouse or something."

He stares at me, and I can tell he isn't convinced.

"Don't worry about it," I tell him, hoping to ease his concerns. "I'm sure everything's fine, Dad hasn't suddenly turned into this monster and even if he did, there's no way Mom would stand for any of it. Two people can't just change their whole personalities overnight. And a house like this is *bound* to have mice."

He continues to stare at me.

"Wanna watch me struggle to get to the door?" I ask, hoping to cheer him up.

He shrugs.

Adjusting myself on the crutches, I get ready to traverse the couple of meters to the doorway. "This might not be pretty," I point out, and then I wait for him to say something. "Then again," I add, "when is *anything* I do pretty, right?" I wait for him to laugh, but he's just staring down at the floor. For my brother to miss an opportunity to make fun of me is unusual. Figuring I just have to get on with things, I take a deep breath, focus for a moment, and then put just the slightest amount of weight on my right leg, just enough to send a shudder of pain up through all the cracked bones.

I let out a gasp of pain.

Scott doesn't laugh this time.

And then I shuffle forward, scratching the leg of my left crutch against the wooden floorboards and, in the process, producing a sound not unlike fingernails being drawn down a chalkboard.

Scott winces and puts his hands over his ears.

Glancing at the floor, I see with a hint of satisfaction that I've carved a faint line in the wood.

"Well," I mutter, feeling the sting of under-used muscles in my shoulders, "I guess I won't be able to sneak up on anyone with these."

After taking another deep breath, I shuffle forward again, and this time the scratching sound is even louder. Finally, almost unbelievably, I reach the doorway and lean against the frame for a moment, before peering around the edge and looking along the bare corridor. To my surprise, I find that nothing has changed since I was carried up to my room three days ago.

"Huh," I mutter, "I thought Mom and Dad were gonna start decorating this place." I look back at Scott. "Are they starting downstairs instead?"

He shakes his head.

"Haven't they started *at all*?" I ask.

He shakes his head again.

"So what *have* they been doing?"

"I don't know," he replies, "just... Dad seems to be watching Mom a lot, like he wants to see what she's doing all the time. It's like he doesn't want her to be alone."

"Dad's way too laid-back to be like that," I point out.

He shrugs.

"None of this sounds quite right," I continue. "I haven't seen Dad today, but yesterday he seemed his usual, happy-go-lucky self. I mean, he was a little snappy when it got late, but that's understandable."

"Then Mom had that nightmare," Scott points out.

"Has she told you anything about it?"

He shakes his head.

"Has she told *Dad* anything about it?"

"I think they were talking about it earlier. When I walked into the hallway, they stopped but... Dad looked angry."

Figuring that what he's saying doesn't make much sense, I glance down at the side of the door-frame and spot the words 'Annie's room' carved crudely into the wood. The lettering is basic and almost infantile.

"So did you do this or not?" I ask.

He cranes his neck to see what I mean. "No," he says after a moment. "That wasn't me. Was it you?"

"How would *I* do have managed to do it?" I ask. "No, it must have been the other -" I stop myself just in time, before I can mention the *other* Annie, the one who disappeared seventy-one years ago. Staring at the carving now, it's more than a little creepy to think of my namesake standing in this exact doorway one day and scratching her name into the wood. For a moment, I try to imagine what she was like, and I can't shake the feeling that since Mom and Dad haven't started decorating yet, the house is probably more or less in the same state it was in all those years ago. Looking out to the landing, I try to imagine the other Annie running from her murderous parents, but the image falls apart when I realize I can't possibly imagine what could have driven two people to murder their own daughter.

"I don't like this house," Scott says suddenly.

I turn to him. "I've barely seen beyond the end of my own -"

Before I can finish, my left crutch shifts, slipping across the floorboards too fast for me to correct my position. I try to grab hold of the door-frame but it's far too late and, instead, I tumble forward, crashing into the end of my bed and letting out a yelp of pain as I over-extend my right leg. I immediately slip off the side of the bed and hit the floor, banging my leg again and gasping as I feel a jolting pain in the bone, racing up through all the cracks. Seconds later, before I even have a chance to get to my feet, I can already hear frantic steps racing up the stairs and finally my father appears in the doorway.

"What the hell is going on in here?" he asks, his eyes filled with shock.

"I didn't do anything!" Scott shouts, drawing his knees up as if to make himself as small as possible. He's scared.

"I'm fine," I splutter, even though – as I try and fail to haul myself up onto the bed – it's clear that I'm not fine at all. Even though I don't want to ask, I'm relieved when my father grabs hold of me and pulls me forward, and then he rolls me over and drags me all the way onto the bed before taking a look at the casts on my legs. To be honest, he seems much rougher than before, as if he's annoyed.

"Are you completely crazy?" he hisses, examining the plaster before stopping when he gets to the lower part of my right leg. "There's a crack here."

"I'm sorry," I reply, leaning back with tears of frustration in my eyes, "I just wanted to get out of this goddamn room! I'm going crazy in here!"

"Well," he continues, "you've probably slowed your recovery down now. Does it hurt?"

"No," I lie.

"Annie, be honest."

"No more than usual."

He touches my bare toes. "Can you feel that?"

"Yes!" I reply, starting to feel increasingly impatient with my own body.

"I should call the doctor," he mutters, "but... We'll see how it goes."

Wiping the tears from my eyes, I prop myself up on my elbows and watch as he continues to examine my casts. Dad has always been quick to call a doctor whenever anything happens, so it seems odd that this time he's not going to bother. It's not that I *want* a doctor to come, but at the same time, I want my father to be his usual self, especially after everything Scott was saying earlier.

"It hurts a *little*," I tell him, hoping to nudge him back to his normal self.

"I'm sure it's fine."

"But if the cast is cracked -"

"It's only a hairline."

"But -"

"Annie!" he snaps, glaring at me with barely-concealed anger. "Just stop! I can see your cast properly, which is more than you can claim. Trust me, there's only the faintest of hairline fractures, and it's obvious your leg isn't too badly damaged." He pauses, before taking a step back and seeming to reset himself slightly, becoming slightly more like his usual self. "I don't want you trying to get out of bed like this again, okay?" He picks my crutches up from the floor. "These are going to be kept well away until *I* decide you're ready for them."

"Can I try my wheelchair instead?" I ask. "I'd at least like to roll around for a while."

"You wouldn't be able to get down the stairs."

"But -"

"You need bed-rest," he continues, "and that's what you'll get, even if I have to tie you down."

"I need the toilet," Scott says, climbing down from the chair and hurrying out the door. It's clear that he just wants to get away from Dad, and a moment later I hear his bedroom door slamming shut.

"I'm not going to tie you down," Dad adds, almost as if he was truly considering that option for a moment. "Annie, you need to consider your health. If I have to lock the door to your room, then -"

"No!" I blurt out, suddenly panicked by the idea. "Please don't do that, Dad, I swear I'll stay in bed!"

He eyes me with caution for a moment. "Well, you'd better. It's not so bad in this room, is it?"

"It's boring as hell."

"Then you'll appreciate things more when you're up and about, won't you?"

"Where's Mom?" I ask. "Can you send her up when she gets back from wherever she's gone?"

"She hasn't gone anywhere," he replies, heading to the door. "She's downstairs, reading."

I frown, surprised that she didn't come with him when they heard me fall.

"Well, can you get her to come up?" I ask, but he just walks away and a moment later I hear him heading downstairs. "Dad?" I call after him. "Did you hear me?"

Sighing, I lean back as he leaves the room. There are still tears in my eyes, mostly due to frustration at my own miserable failure. If I'd just managed to stay on the crutches, I could have proved to them that I can get about, but I guess maybe I tried a day or two too early. I swear, sometimes I feel like I'm never going to get out of this stupid room.

CHAPTER TWELVE

Seventy-one years ago

WATCHING MYSELF IN THE mirror, I reach back and start to tie my hair. I know it's a little vain to spend time bothering about my personal appearance, but I feel the need to look more grown-up. After all, I'm no longer a child and it won't do to look like one, so I have begun to experiment with various subtle changes. Fortunately, Mother's dresses fit me rather well, and I intend to take them in a few inches at the waist. My hair, meanwhile, looks much better when it's tied back.

I swear, just these few simple changes make me look ten years older, perhaps even more.

Once I'm certain that I look my best, I head out of my room and down the stairs. It's still early and I intend to reorganize the kitchen, to make it fit my needs a little better. All last night, I lay in bed planning some alterations I intend to make around the house, and although I haven't mentioned any of these out loud yet to Father, I'm quite certain that they will meet no resistance. After all, every single one of them is rooted in common sense and -

Stopping suddenly in the kitchen doorway, I stare in horror at the sight of Mother working at the sink, washing breakfast dishes.

Father, at the table, glances at me for a moment with somber eyes before looking back down at his plate.

"What..." I pause, convinced that this has to be some kind of mistake. "What's happening?"

"Your Mother has come back up," Father mutters. "She's learned her lesson."

I watch as Mother limps to the cupboard and sets a plate on the shelf. She has to tilt her head, as if she's trying to see out through one of the less scratched parts of her damaged eyes; although it takes a moment, she's able to find a cup on the counter and take it back to the sink. She glances at me, and although there's a great deal of fear in her eyes, there's also some self-satisfaction. She's wearing a proper dress again and her hair is more or less back to its old neatness, but as she starts to wash the cup I can't help but feel she looks like a savage dressed up in civilized clothes. As if to prove that point, she almost knocks a stack of pots over, and it's clear that her damaged eyes make it much harder for her to work. She's still blinking furiously, almost non-stop, as if the scratches are unbearably uncomfortable.

"Father," I continue finally, turning to him with a sense of cold steel in my chest, "you didn't say that -"

"It's done now," he replies. "I made the decision

this morning."

"But -" With tears in my eyes, I start to feel an incandescent rage building through my body. I clench both my fists, filled with the urge to go over and beat Mother back down into the basement, but I know Father would stop me and I also know that I wouldn't get what I want by letting my anger overflow. I take a series of deep breaths in order to stay calm, and as I watch Father eat, I try to work out what I could have done to displease him so much that he would rather have Mother back. He never acted as if I had disappointed him, but clearly I must have done something wrong.

"Annie -" he begins.

"Excuse me," I stammer, turning and hurrying to the bathroom, my eyes already filling with tears.

***

Father is chopping wood and Mother is in the kitchen, and I am sitting on the porch steps. Mild spring sunlight shines down, but I feel sick to my stomach as I watch Father work and hear, from over my shoulder, the sounds of Mother shuffling about in the kitchen. Barely able to see at all, she works so slowly, I feel as if she should just be put out of her misery. The fact that she's trying so hard only makes her even more pitiful.

I hate her.

No, it's more than hate.

I'm repulsed by her. I'm offended by the fact that she exists.

Getting to my feet, I briefly consider going over

to talk to Father some more, to work out what I did wrong and how to set it straight. He's not a man of many words and our conversations are usually brief, but I still feel the urge to make him tell me how I could have been such a disappointment. Those days when Mother was down in the basement were among the happiest of my life, and although I have gone over every moment in my mind a thousand times, I still can't think of a single thing that I did wrong. Perhaps I did not excel at certain duties, but I showed I was keen to learn. Still, by bringing Mother back up, he has rejected me.

Even worse, he has barely spoken to me all morning. He even avoids eye contact.

Perhaps if I were to plead with him...

"Annie," Mother calls out suddenly from the back door. "I need your help."

I shiver at the mere sound of her voice, and at the idea that she should call on me for any kind of help at all. I had begun to make that kitchen mine, yet now she thinks she can reclaim it. Does the woman have no shame at all?

"Annie," she says again. "Come."

Another shiver passes through my body, so intense that I have to squeeze my eyes tight shut and clench my fists just to keep from crying out with rage. I can feel tears welling in my eyes, but I force them back, determined to remain in control of my own body. I will not let this woman beat me.

"Annie! Don't make me tell you again!"

"Coming!" I reply, opening my eyes wide and watching for a moment as Father continues to chop wood. Turning, I walk up the steps toward the back door, my whole body stiff with rage. When I reach the kitchen, I see that Mother has set various pots and pans on the table, along with the ingredients to roast a leg of lamb. She knows that leg of lamb is Father's favorite meal, a luxury we can only afford once or twice a year, and I feel sick to the stomach at the thought of her trying to inveigle herself back into his good books like this.

"I need you to help me," she says, with her back to me as she sets out a block of butter and some herbs. "I can't see more than a few shadows but there's a lot to do, so you must go to the garden and fetch plenty of carrots and parsnips. And two turnips. Those are your father's favorites, you know."

Looking down at the knives on the table, I want nothing more than to drive one of them into her pathetic head.

"After you've brought the vegetables in," she continues, "you must scrub enough potatoes for the three of us and then peel them. Get started on that nice and early, because I intend to roast them very slowly and I don't want dinner to be too late. I'll have more jobs for you after, too, so there's really no time to waste." She turns to me and smiles a cautious, reticent smile, as if she's nervous. Her damaged eyes are staring almost directly at me, the scratches barely visible in the morning light. "I want to make your father happy. I want to give him the best meal he's ever eaten."

I feel a knot of horror in my belly, twisting in disgust at the thought that she thinks she could ever make Father happy. What gives her that right? She's failed enough times, and now it's my turn. I want to crack her head open, but I know I must be patient.

"Annie, you must get started," she adds, turning back to the chopping board. Her hands fumble for the herbs since she can't see them very well. It's almost like watching a child trying to prepare a meal. "There really isn't any time to lose. I haven't told your father that I'm doing any of this, and I'd like to get it started while he's out there working. I'd like it to be a surprise for him."

Stepping over to the table, I pick up the largest carving knife. The leg of lamb is resting on a plate, its skin all stripped away to reveal the sinewy muscle beneath. There are traces of blood on the plate, and at the nearest end the bone has been broken away, revealing a rich seam of marrow running through the center. Mother has already arranged plenty of herbs over the surface, but I reach out and brush them away, feeling as if the meat should be pure when it cooks. Pressing against the leg's muscle, I feel its firm, smooth surface and I think of all the blood still inside. Mother is right, Father *does* love this meal, but it feels wrong that someone like her should be the one who gives it to him. She's trying to buy back his affection, and to my mind this only makes her more pathetic.

Slowly, I slide the knife into the side of the leg, pushing it all the way through and enjoying the sensation. After a moment, I pull it out again.

"Hey!" she says, hurrying over and pushing my hand away from the meat. "You mustn't touch it too much. Have you washed since you were out in the garden?" She peers closer at the meat, as if she's worried

I've dirtied it somehow, but it's clear she can't see properly. She's pretending, doing her best, but she can't even see where I slipped the knife in. "We don't want to contaminate anything, now do we?"

Swallowing hard, I feel as if I might vomit if I have to hear one more word from her pathetic mouth.

"You seem well," I tell her. "Considering."

"Considering what?" she asks. Glancing at me briefly, she lets a sliver of fear into her eyes. "Annie, I really don't have time to stand around talking all day, so you must go to the garden and do as I asked." She waits for a moment, and I can tell that she's trying to hide her nerves. Finally, she points toward the door with a trembling hand. "Annie, go! Now! We're doing this for your father!"

"How would you know what Father likes?" I reply, unable to hold my tongue a moment longer.

"I beg your pardon?"

"You don't know him," I continue. "You don't understand him." Glancing at the window, I see Father in the distance, all the way over on the other side of the lawn, near the trees. I turn back to Mother. "You can't make him happy."

She stares at me with those ugly, scratched eyes. "And you think you're suddenly such an expert, do you?" she asks, her voice filled with disgust. "There's something wrong with you of late, my girl. Something dark and cruel."

I shake my head.

"Did your father sleep in your room while I was in the basement?" she asks. "You don't even have to answer, I know the truth. You're foul, both of you."

"What are you talking about?" I reply, trying to control the urge to last out at her.

"You're very close to him, aren't you?" she continues with a sneer. "Sometimes I wonder if you want to -"

"Liar!" I shout, pushing her in the chest so hard that she stumbles back against one of the cabinets and lets out a gasp of shock. "You filthy, dirty-minded whore!" I continue, slapping the side of her face as hard as I can imagine. "Is that really what you think? I'm just close to Father, that's all! I actually care about him and understand him!"

"Annie," she stammers, "please -"

"You must have the most evil mind," I sneer, "to entertain such awful thoughts."

"I'm sorry," she replies, "perhaps I spoke out of place..."

"Perhaps?" I ask, stepping closer to her with the knife still in my hand. "You don't understand Father and you certainly don't understand me! You have the heart and soul of a common beast!"

She turns to go back over to the counter, and her trembling hands reach for a bottle of oil.

"My word, girl," she says after a moment, her voice trembling with fear, "you must learn to do as you're told. I never intended to insinuate anything untoward, I was merely remarking upon some of the changes I've observed in you of late." She pours oil into a pan. "You must admit, you've been rather highly-strung."

And that's when I can stand her no longer.

Hurrying over to her, I grab her by the neck and pull her toward me, before slicing the knife deep into her back until the tip pokes out from the front of her dress. To keep her from crying out, I place my left hand over her mouth; she tries to scream, but I squeeze her lips tight shut, pinching them tight so that she can't make any more noise than a muffled murmur. At the same time, I twist the knife in her back and feel the blade grinding against her ribs, but still she struggles so I pull the knife out and slide it in again, further up this time, closer to where her heart should be. It feels exactly like when I put the knife into the leg of lamb a moment ago.

"You," I whisper directly into her ear, "are nothing but a whore with a mind full of foul and impure thoughts."

I can feel saliva leaking out from between her lips, onto my fingers as I continue to hold her mouth closed, but something seems to have changed; whereas a few seconds ago she was struggling constantly, now her struggle seems to be in a series of short, sharp jerks, punctuated by moments of rest. I twist the knife in her back again, having to briefly let go of the handle so I can adjust my grip and turn it some more, and such is the force of my anger that I feel the blade once again grinding against her splitting ribs. Pulling her further back, I feel as if I should whisper something more into her ear, but no words really seem necessary. Perhaps, if a woman is forced to kill her own mother, the task should be completed in silence. Instead of saying a word more, I slide the knife out and then push it back in, determined to find her heart. This time, her body shudders once and then remains tense, and I feel as if she's not trying quite so hard to cry out. I wait, counting the seconds as they pass, before she starts to fall limp in my grasp and I realize that if I wasn't holding her up, she'd have collapsed by now.

Looking over at the window, I see Father still working at the far end of the garden, close to the line of trees.

Mother hasn't twitched for fully five or six seconds now, so I slowly let go of her lips. As soon as I do so, a gulp of blood slops out onto my fingers and then runs down her chin, splattering onto the counter. I pull the knife out of her back and finally look down, and I'm shocked by the sheer amount of blood that has soaked not only the back of her dress but also the front of mine, and my right hand too. I was so focused on holding her still and keeping her quiet, I had no idea that blood was not only covering us both, but had also begun to splatter down onto the kitchen floor. Taking a few steps back, I keep hold of Mother's neck and feel a burst of relief when she slumps in my arms. I cannot imagine, from the feel of her, that there can be much life left in her body at all. I set her down on the floor and look into her scratched eyes, and although they're perfectly still, I can't help wondering if there's still just a flicker of consciousness remaining, watching me as it dwindles to nothing.

I open my mouth, still feeling as if I should say something, but no words come. What words could possibly be appropriate at a time like this? Better, I think, to just let her slip away. She certainly doesn't deserve to be comforted.

I don't know the exact moment when she dies, but after a couple of minutes I check for a pulse on the side of her neck and find nothing. I check the other side, just to be sure, and then I check her wrists, but still there's nothing. Worried that she might be trying to fool me, I take the knife and drive the tip into her cheek until the blade has passed through into her mouth and pierced her tongue, but she doesn't react at all. Pulling the knife out and sitting back, I realize that I'm ever so slightly out of breath, but I can't hold back a smile at the realization that Mother is finally, and permanently, out of the way.

In fact, I even allow myself a brief, contained laugh.

After a few minutes, I get to my feet and look down at all the blood that has soaked into my dress from Mother's back. Lifting the dress over my head, I drop it to the floor and then glance out the window, to make sure that Father is still working. Slipping out of the rest of my clothes, which are also stained with blood and which I must surely throw away, I step over Mother's body and head to the bathroom, where I draw some water into the bath and take a moment to clean myself. The water is cold, of course, and I start shivering a little, but I absolutely *must* get clean as quickly as possible. I even scrub under my fingernails and wash my hair, and finally after about half an hour I climb from the bath and dry myself, before hurrying upstairs and going to my room, where some of Mother's dresses are still hanging in the closet. I look out the window to check that Father is still working, before slipping into one of the dresses and then looking into the mirror so that I can fix my hair. It takes a while to get everything sorted but I want to look my best, so I don't rush. The worst thing in the world would be for Father to see my when I'm not all fixed up.

By the time I get back down to the kitchen, it must have been an hour at least since Mother died. She's still where I left her, and her dead eyes are still staring up at the ceiling. Stepping closer, I look down and see that the scratches from the sandpaper were deeper than I'd realized, and it's hard to believe she could even get from one room to another without bumping into things. Still, this isn't the time to start feeling pity. I have to get on with the job of making this roast, although first I need to clear the kitchen.

Heading out to the porch, I watch for a moment as Father continues to work. I can't hide a faint smile as I make my way across the lawn, and my heart is pounding in my chest as I reach him. At first he doesn't look at me, preferring to keep chopping wood, but finally he turns and waits for me to speak.

"Is something wrong?" he asks finally.

"No," I tell him, "nothing's wrong. But we need to bury Mother."

CHAPTER THIRTEEN

Today

"MOM!" I SHOUT, SITTING up in bed and listening to the sound of something bumping downstairs. "Mom, what's wrong? Mom!"

It's midday and while Dad and Scott are out in town, Mom stayed behind to keep me company and get started painting the front room. With no internet and no TV, I've spent the morning reading more of the old books that Mom found from her boxes, while waiting with increasing impatience for her to find *my* boxes with *my* books. And then, about thirty seconds ago, I heard the sound of someone banging into things in one of the rooms below.

"Mom!" I call out again. "Are you okay?"

I wait.

Silence.

"I'm fine!" she calls back suddenly, sounding

distracted. "It's nothing, Annie, really."

"What happened?"

"Nothing!"

"More nothing, huh?"

I wait for a reply, but none comes.

Frowning, I listen to the sound of her moving things around in the room directly below. I guess maybe she's been shifting furniture and knocked something over, but for the past couple of days Mom has been acting increasingly strangely, and this morning she seemed positively jumpy. I've tried asking her what's wrong and she always says it's nothing to worry about, but she also tells me not to mention anything to Dad, which I definitely take to be a sign that I should be concerned. Even now, listening to her clattering about down there, I can't shake the feeling that she's hiding something. I've started to lose count of how often I've heard that word 'nothing' lately.

A few minutes later, I hear footsteps coming up the stairs and Mom comes into my room with a sandwich on a plate and a glass of milk.

"I thought you might be hungry," she says with a forced smile.

"You're not fooling me, you know," I tell her as she sets the plate and glass down on my bedside table.

"What's that, sweetheart?"

"I said you're not fooling me. Something's wrong."

She sighs.

"Something's *wrong*," I say again, figuring that I need to force the matter a little. "You can either tell me now or tell me later, but we both know you *will* tell me at some point, so..." I pat the bed next to my right leg. "Spill the beans."

She stares at me for a moment, before making her way around the bed and looking out the window. She seems worried.

"Have you seen something?" I ask finally.

I want her to tell me that no, of course she hasn't seen anything, but instead she glances at me and I can immediately tell that I'm on the money.

"What did you see?"

She hesitates, as if she's worried I'll laugh at her.

"Was it that woman again?" I ask.

"I..." She pauses. "What woman?"

"You know, the -"

"Describe her to me," she continues. "The one you thought you saw the other day from this window."

"She was wearing a white dress and she had black hair," I reply. "That's really all I could see. She was standing out there, looking down at a spot on the lawn. I didn't see her face or anything."

She stares at me for a moment, before looking back out the window. I swear, the cold morning light is making her look so pale right now.

"Where did you see her?" I ask.

"Annie..."

"*Where* did you *see* her?"

She continues to look out the window for a moment.

"The basement," she says finally, her voice so faint it's almost impossible to hear.

"Tell me exactly what happened."

"It's silly, really..." She looks back at the door, as if she's worried we might be overheard. "Your father doesn't like me going down there," she continues, turning to me. "He says it's not safe, something about exposed wires." She sighs. "I don't even know if that's true, but he's got the place locked up like Fort Knox, and then yesterday morning I had to go down there to take a look at the fuse box. Your father was out and I couldn't wait, so I found the spare keys and..." Her voice trails off for a moment. "There are no lights down there," she explains, "and I only had the light from my phone, but you know where the fuse box is, right?"

I shake my head.

"Of course not," she mutters. "You've barely seen outside this room. Well, it's about halfway along the basement's far wall. There was light coming down the stairs from the open door, obviously, but it was still kind of creepy being down there alone. Not that I was getting paranoid or anything, I definitely didn't get worked up and imagine the whole thing." She pauses again. "I was replacing one of the fuses when I heard a noise. At first it seemed like something scraping across the concrete floor, but after a moment it seemed more like it was coming from the ceiling, like someone... So I looked over, thinking it was a rat or something, but I didn't see anything. I got back to work, and even though I heard the sound a few more times, I told myself it was nothing. And then..."

"Then what?"

"There's a meter on the fuse box case, with a

glass panel. I kept checking it to see if the dial was turning properly, I could see my own reflection in the glass but that didn't really matter, and then one time when I looked..."

I wait for her to continue.

"What did you see?" I ask.

"There was... I *thought* there was someone standing right behind me. A woman in a white dress, with black hair, and as I stared at the reflection I saw her hand reaching up to my shoulder." She reaches up and touches her right shoulder. "I was too shocked and scared to move, I just stood there and watched as her hand moved closer and closer. I stayed completely still until..."

"Until what?"

She pauses. "I felt her."

"What do you mean, you *felt* her?"

"I felt her hand on my shoulder," she continues, indicating a spot at the side of her neck. "Right here. Just lightly, but... I didn't just see something, Annie, I felt it. It touched me!"

"Did you turn around?"

She nods.

"And?"

"And there was nothing. It was gone, but I swear..." She shivers as she looks at her shoulder. "It's probably nothing, but that combined with the nightmare -"

"Tell me about the nightmare."

She shakes her head.

"Why not?"

"Because it's all just dumb," she continues, clearly exasperated. "It was just a creepy dream about a woman with scratched eyes -"

"Scratched eyes?"

"Like..." She points at her own eyes. "They were both scratched to hell, with lots of little lines crisscrossing and... It's not something I really want to think about, I've only just started to get it out of my system." She pauses, as if she wants to say something else but can't quite get it out. "She was staring at me with this intensity, like she expected me to know something or do something or..."

Her voice trails off.

"Mom," I say finally, "are you starting to worry that this house is -"

"No," she says firmly.

"But if it's -"

"Don't say the word."

"I don't believe in ghosts," I continue, "I mean not really, but if *you* think the place is haunted, then that's something we should talk about." I wait for a reply. "Has anyone else seen anything?"

"I don't think so," she replies. "Your father's being a little odd, but I think that's just the stress of the move. Scott seems quiet, but he's probably picking it up from me. Your father was worried that might happen, maybe he was right." She pauses again. "What about you, Annie? Have you seen or heard anything, stuck up here in your room?"

"Not really," I tell her. "Not apart from that woman I saw from the window."

"She was probably just one of the neighbors."

"I hope so."

"Mom," I continue, "do you know about -" I stop myself just in time, figuring that maybe this isn't the right moment to tell her about the murder that took place here seventy-one years ago. Dad said she's better off knowing, and I think he might be right. "You should talk to Dad about this," I tell her. "Seriously, don't let him brush you off. If you've got concerns, you need to air them."

"This has gone far enough," she continues, forcing a smile as she gets to her feet and pats my knee. "Eat your lunch and I'll be up later, we can watch a film before your father and Scott get home. Does that sound like a good deal?"

"Sure," I reply, feeling as if she needs the company as much as I do. As she heads out of the room, I can't shake the feeling that she's way, *way* more on edge than I've ever seen her before, but I honestly don't know how to help. Everything she told me can be explained away as the result of her being spooked and a little impressionable, but then there's the woman I saw from the window. Leaning across the bed, I look out and watch the lawn for a moment, half expecting to see someone, but of course there isn't a soul out there.

Not at the moment, anyway.

CHAPTER FOURTEEN

Seventy-one years ago

IT'S ANOTHER BEAUTIFUL JULY day, and Father works from dawn 'til dusk. Mostly he chops firewood, but he also checks traps in the forest and repairs a hole in the barn door. It's not that I'm checking up on him; I simply spot him from time to time when I glance out the kitchen window, and I see him going about his business in the distance.

    He's happy.

    I'm happy.

    I can't help but smile.

    For my part, I have a great deal to learn. Mother always ran the house reasonably well, even if she cut corners from time to time, so I have to get up to speed before Father notices any differences. I want him to see that he can rely on me. I've already spent the morning reorganizing the kitchen and giving it a good clean, including the spots that Mother evidently missed. Working hard and fast, I got that job done by midday and now I've moved on to the rest of the house, going from room to room and fixing everything methodically. Truth be told, I've fallen into something of a daze, working almost like a machine, and by the time I'm done upstairs I find that it's almost four in the afternoon, which means I must start preparing dinner.

This all feels so right, as if it's what I'm meant to be doing.

The one strange thing is that every so often, I find little patches of water, as if something has dripped onto the floor. There appear to be no holes in the roof, and I'm certainly not spilling, and in some cases the water even appears in spots that I *know* I've already cleaned today. On one occasion, I even see water smeared against the wall in the hallway, as if someone wet brushed against the wood, but such a thing is quite impossible.

I even start to feel as if -

But no, I'm just letting my thoughts run on. Father is in the garden and I'm quite alone in the house.

As I head along the landing, I stop and look at the words 'Annie's room' carved into one of the doorframes. That awful night, when Mother pushed Father to such great anger, feels as if it took place a hundred lifetimes ago. Smiling, I run a fingertip against the deep grooves that Father cut into the wood, tracing each of the letters one by one until I've completed both words, and I whisper them out loud.

"Annie's room."

The irony, of course, is that now Mother has left us, there's really no need to have this little notice anymore, but I feel it should remain. Not as a warning, not any longer; more as a reminder, and a statement of great pride.

Heading downstairs, I glance out the kitchen window and smile once again as I see Father carrying a heavy load of wood to the barn. He puts too much weight on his shoulders, of course, but then again I suppose he knows what he's doing. He's a strong, capable man who has been working hard on this land since he was just a child, and I wouldn't dare interfere and tell him how things should be run. The house is my domain, now that I've taken it over from Mother, and I must focus on the tasks that fall to me. I can be quite happy like this.

No, I can be *more* than happy.

I can live my whole life in this daze of usefulness.

I belong here. Mother never understood, of course. She ascribed base, lowly motives to my actions, and she allowed her foul mind to imagine all sorts of perversions and disgusting acts. It's typical that she thought like that, but at least she's gone now.

This is a pure and happy house.

Chaste and calm.

Later that night, after dinner has been eaten and tidied away, Father goes and sits in his armchair, and I take him his usual glass of whiskey. In the old days, when Mother was around, these moments were often the most tense, since he would often be brooding and thinking of Mother's many mistakes. No longer. He seems more relaxed, albeit a little pensive, and for a short while I'm not really sure what I should do. Finally, aware that all my tasks are done for the day, and feeling aches and pains in my joints, I make my way over to the chair and settle on the floor. I lean toward Father and set my face against the side of his trousers, the way I would in the old days, and I look up at his face as it's caught by the hearth's flickering light.

He glances down at me briefly, before turning and looking back at the fire.

Something is definitely on his mind.

No matter. I shall simply wait here, happily, until he decides that it's time to retire for the night. I have been useful to him today and made him proud, and that's really at my first proper attempt. I cannot imagine how much better I will be at housekeeping once I've had more practice, but I know one thing for certain:

We're much better off without Mother, and my room is now Father's room too.

Still, as I sit here, I can't shake the feeling that I'm being watched. I turn and look across the dark room, with only the light from a single candle flickering in the corner. There's no-one in the doorway, but I feel as if perhaps there *was* someone there just a moment ago, just before I looked. I tell myself that I'm being foolish, but just as I'm about to turn back to Father I realize I can see more splashes of water on the floor, right in the doorway, glistening in the candlelight. I hold my breath for a moment, trying to work out what could possibly be happening, but I figure I should just keep my concerns to myself and deal with the problem without disturbing Father.

A moment later I hear the back door bumping shut in the breeze. Somehow, I must have left it open.

CHAPTER FIFTEEN

Today

"WHAT THE HELL WERE you thinking?" Dad hisses as he and Mom hurry upstairs. "Why would you say something like that in front of Scott?"

"I didn't know he was standing right behind me," she replies, clearly keeping her voice down so Scott won't hear them from downstairs. "Come on, I'd never start talking about that sort of thing when he's around!"

"It's bad enough -"

Dad stops suddenly, and a moment later he appears in my doorway and grabs the handle. "Hey," he says with a fake smile, "I'm just going to close this for a moment, okay?"

"Why?" I ask.

"Just for a moment," he replies, pulling the door shut. A moment later, I hear him and Mom going into the bedroom next door, and I hear another door shutting.

They're blatantly arguing, but although I can still hear their muffled voices, I can't quite make out what they're saying. Reaching over, I loosen the latch on the window and then slide the panel up, and since their bedroom window is open now, I can hear them again.

"He's an impressionable boy," Dad is saying, his voice filled with frustration. "Annie's not much better, they're both still kids and if you keep on like this you're going to give them ideas!"

"Scott said he saw -"

"Scott's just copying you!"

"No he's not, Annie saw something too!"

"Oh, *Annie*?" he replies, sounding distinctly unimpressed. "You mean our daughter, who's spent the past few days sitting in bed with plenty of time to let her imagination run rampant?"

"Thanks," I mutter.

She sighs. "I want to look into the history of the house some more, I want to find out if anything bad ever happened here. You said the place was empty when we bought it, maybe there's a reason for that?"

"You're being irrational."

"We all saw that woman!" she continues. "I saw her, Scott saw her, Annie saw her!"

"Well I sure as hell didn't see her!"

"There's something going on here," she tells him. "It seems to be centered around the basement and the kitchen. It's not just the woman we saw, either. There have been other things."

"Oh, really?" he replies, with a hint of sarcasm in his voice. "Go on then, tell me these other things." I can just imagine him right now, folding his arms across his chest in that I'm-smarter-than-you way of his.

"Sometimes I feel like there's someone in the kitchen with me," she continues. "I turn around and I don't see anyone, but it's almost like someone's watching me while I'm in there, someone who hates me. I know that sounds crazy, but once or twice over the past week there's been this really palpable sense of pure anger and disgust, and it seems to be directed right at me! Plus, sometimes when that happens, I find patches of water on the floor. I know that sounds insane, but it's really happening!"

"So now the ghost is targeting you? Seriously?"

"I didn't say that."

"More or less," he replies. "What about the basement? What do you *think* you saw down there?"

"I told you, the reflection of the -"

"Anything else?"

"I don't -"

"I'm not going to let you ruin this for us," he hisses. "Jesus Christ, we moved out here because *you* wanted to bring the kids up in a rural location. I was perfectly happy in New York, but you insisted on coming out here, and now apparently the place isn't good enough because there's some kind of ghost haunting the kitchen and the basement? Are you seriously pulling this on me? Are you so completely irrational that you can't see how crazy this is?"

"I'm not trying to -"

"Let's go take a look," he adds. "Come on, we'll go to the basement and see if there's anything down there."

"You're the one who keeps it locked all the time!"

"Well now I'm unlocking it!"

I hear the sound of a scuffle.

"Hey!" Mum hisses.

"You're coming with me!" Dad replies, and a moment later there's a faint bump. I hear footsteps out on the landing, almost as if Dad's forcing Mom to the stairs, and then I hear them heading down to the hallway. There's no way Dad would *ever* get violent, but he sure as hell doesn't sound like himself right now, and a moment later I hear a bump in the room below, as if the door to the basement was just pulled open. Dad's obviously taking Mom down there, but I hate the idea that he's acting like such an ass.

Instinctively, I try to get up, having momentarily forgotten that I'm stuck here thanks to my stupid legs. Letting out a gasp of frustration, I sit back and try to work out what I can do, and then I spot Mom's phone still sitting on the bedside table. I quickly bring up Dad's number and wait for a connection, while running through what I'm going to say to him.

"Hang on," he spits as soon as he answers, clearly in the middle of arguing with Mom. "What's going on? Who -"

"It's me," I tell him. "Dad, what are you doing? I heard your argument just now, you don't know what you're talking about!"

"Annie -"

"You have to listen to Mom!" I continue. "You

might not believe her, but you have to listen to her! She's not crazy!"

"Don't butt in on things you don't understand," he replies, his clipped tones sounding colder than usual. "When we're done down here, I'll bring you something to eat and -"

"I don't care about that! I want you to listen to Mom!"

"And I want you to mind your own business!"

"Dad -"

"You don't get to call me and lecture me like this," he snaps, interrupting me. "Do you hear me? You don't know anything, Annie! You're just a child!"

"I know something's going on in this house!"

"You don't even know what this house looks like outside of your room," he replies dismissively. "You only know what you hear from up there and what people tell you, so don't act like you've got some great perspective. Now if you don't mind, I'm talking to your mother about something and when I want to hear your opinion, I'll come up to your little room and ask for it!"

"Hey," I reply, "you don't -"

Before I can get another word out, I realize he's cut the call. I immediately try to ring back, only to get put straight through to voice-mail, which I guess means he's turned the phone off. Filled with frustration, I toss Mom's phone aside and look down at the floor, toward the spot that I think is above the kitchen.

"You're being an ass!" I shout, loud enough that he should be able to hear me even down in the basement. "What the hell's wrong with you? Mom, tell him to go to hell!"

"Dad's different," Scott says suddenly.

Turning, I see that he's standing in the doorway. I freeze, seeing that all the hints of fear from the past few days have now blossomed across his face.

"What do you mean?" I ask, sitting up but wincing a little as I feel a sharp pain in my legs.

"He's angry all the time," he continues, taking a step into the room. "He was sitting in the kitchen earlier and Mom was making dinner, and Dad was talking to himself."

"I..." Pausing, I realize that no matter how absurd that idea sounds, Scott seems completely genuine. "Talking to himself *how*, exactly?"

"Really quietly," he replies, stopping at the end of my bed. "Like, mumbling under his breath." He has that expression I remember from when we were both younger, the expression he always wore after a nightmare had made him soil the bed, as if true fear has gripped his soul. "I was watching him. I couldn't hear more than a whisper, but his lips were definitely moving. He kept looking over at the back door, too, like he expected to see someone there."

"Dad doesn't talk to himself," I point out. "Only crazy people talk to themselves."

"Does that mean Dad's crazy?" he asks, with tears in his eyes.

"It means -"

Before I can reply, I hear a creaking sound nearby and I turn just in time to see my bedroom door swinging shut, slamming into the frame so hard that the wood shudders.

"Who did that?" I ask, scooching myself back in the bed. "Scott, open the door and see who's out there!"

He shakes his head.

"Scott, do it! Hurry!"

He hesitates, before stepping toward the door. I can tell he's scared, but to his credit he turns the handle and pushes the door open, before leaning out to look along the landing.

"Who's there?" I ask.

He pauses, before turning back to me. "No-one," he says quietly, his voice trembling.

"It must have been -" I stop for a moment, realizing I can hear Dad still haranguing Mom down in the basement. "Is the window open by the top of the stairs?" I ask, hoping that maybe a gust of wind was responsible.

Scott shakes his head.

"Okay," I continue, patting the side of the bed, "come sit with me."

"Annie -"

"Just come sit," I tell him, and this time he hurries over. It's been a long time since I treated my little brother as anything other than a pre-pubescent annoyance, but I quickly put an arm around his shoulder and feel that he's trembling. "It's going to be okay," I continue, watching the half-open door with a hint of fear in my chest. "Mom and Dad are just arguing, people argue all the time."

"Mom and Dad didn't argue like this in the old house," he points out.

"Moving's stressful."

"Dad didn't talk to himself in the old house, either."

"No, but -" I pause as I realize there seems to be someone on the landing. I can't *see* them, or *hear* them, but as I stare at the door I feel overwhelmed for a moment by the sense that someone's just out of sight, listening to us. "Don't worry about Dad," I continue, forcing myself to look down at Scott as Mom and Dad continue to argue in the basement. "He'll calm down soon, and if he doesn't, Mom'll put him in his place. She won't let him act like an ass for -"

Suddenly the door slams shut again, more violently than before, and this time it clicks and *stays* shut.

"Who did that?" Scott asks, turning to me.

"No-one," I reply, "it's just..." Pausing, I realize that both times the door slammed shut, one of us had just said something bad about Dad. Still, that's probably a coincidence. There's no more shouting from downstairs, so I reach out and give Scott a hug. "They've stopped arguing. That's good. Mom probably..." I take a deep breath, watching the door, wondering whether I should test my theory. "Mom..." I take another deep breath. This is crazy, but... "Mom probably just pointed out to him that he was being an idiot." I wait, still watching the door, waiting for something to happen. If my theory's right, then saying something bad about Dad should trigger something else. "I mean, he *is* being an idiot," I continue, trying not to let the fear into my voice. "Dad's... Dad's just a big old -"

Suddenly the door swings open, but this time Dad steps through, having apparently hurried up the stairs.

"Why are you being like this?" I ask.

"Come on, Scott," he says firmly, "you need to come down and eat your dinner."

Scott turns to me, and I can see he doesn't want to go alone. Still, it's not like I can hop down off the bed and follow.

"Why don't you all eat up here with me?" I ask, turning to Dad. "Get Mom to come up too."

"Your mother's taking a time-out," he replies.

"What's that supposed to mean?"

"It means she's thinking about things."

"Why?" I wait for him to explain, but he reaches across the bed and grabs Scott's arm. "Dad, what the hell are you on about? Since when does Mom have to take a time-out for anything? She's not a child!"

"She'll come back up when she's had time to consider her ways," he replies, trying to pull Scott off the bed.

"Come back up? What -" I pause for a moment, feeling a slowly creeping sense of shock. "Is she still in the basement?"

"Just for now."

"Why's she in the basement?" I ask. "Dad, why is Mom down there?"

"She needs some time alone to think," he replies, still trying to pull Scott off the bed. "She's acting very irrationally and I think it'd be good for her to calm down and focus on getting her head straight. I'll let her back up in an hour or two."

"*Let* her back up?" I watch as Scott finally climbs off the bed and allows Dad to lead him toward the door. "Did you lock Mom in the basement?" I ask, unable to believe what I'm hearing. "Dad, are you -"

"She needed it!" he shouts, turning to me with anger in his eyes. "You heard her! She was out of control!"

"You can't lock her away!"

"Scott," he continues, looking down at my brother, "wait downstairs."

Scott turns to me.

"It'll be okay," I tell him, before looking back at Dad as Scott steps out onto the landing. "Dad, you can't seriously be telling me you locked Mom in the basement. Please, tell me I'm misunderstanding, because that's insane!"

"It's for her own good. She's acting like a child." He reaches down and takes Mom's phone from my bed. "She shouldn't have given you this, either."

"Why are you doing this?" I ask. "You're acting like some kind of neanderthal, you're -"

"Annie!" Scott yells.

I turn just in time to see his shocked face as the door slams shut again, leaving him out on the landing as the door-frame rattles once again.

"It's you," I whisper, horrified as I turn to Dad. "What's really happening here? Dad, this house -"

"There's nothing wrong with this house," he continues, marching across the room and pulling the door open to reveal a terrified Scott on the other side.

"Go downstairs now!" he shouts, before turning back to me. Behind him, Scott turns and hurries away. "Annie," Dad says firmly, "I told your mother that she was in danger of influencing you and your brother, and right now you're just validating all my concerns. Everyone in this house just needs to calm down, step back, and gain a little perspective."

"What are you going to do," I reply, "lock me in my room?"

He pauses, before taking a step back. "I don't need to lock you in, really, do I? You're kind of stuck already." With that, he swings the door shut, leaving me alone.

"Hey!" I shout, filled with frustration but unable to do a goddamn thing about it. "Get back here!"

I wait, but all I hear is Dad heading downstairs.

"You can't do this!" I yell, almost shaking as anger builds in my chest. "You don't have any right! What are you, some kind of complete moron?"

Suddenly I spot something moving out the corner of my eye. I turn just in time to see the faintest flash of motion in the mirror above the dresser, but I'm too late to see exactly what it is. I wait, my heart pounding as I hold my breath, but the room remains still and calm.

From downstairs, there's the sound of Dad arguing with Scott. He doesn't even sound like himself anymore.

CHAPTER SIXTEEN

Seventy-one years ago

I HEAR THE CAR before I see it. While sitting on the porch steps, scrubbing potatoes for dinner, I look over at the dirt road that leads away from the house and I realize there's a vehicle headed this way. Trying not to panic, I get to my feet just as a dark car rounds the corner at the edge of the forest, and I immediately recognize it as a police vehicle.

It's getting closer and closer with each passing second.

Trying not to panic, I start wiping my hands on my apron. Father is out in the forest, doing some work down by the lake, and although my initial reaction is to go into the house and refuse to answer the door, I'm sure the driver of the car must have seen me by now. As I try to work out what to do, I watch the car turning into the yard and finally it comes to a stop just a short distance away. I've never seen a car up close before, so the sight is somewhat shocking. A moment later, the door opens and a police officer steps out. He's smiling, which somehow feels wrong.

"Is this the Garrett residence?" he asks.

"I..." Taking a deep breath, I try to stay calm. "It is."

"Is Mr. Garrett at home?"

"He's not," I reply, as the officer steps around the car and comes closer. "He's out, he'll be out all day."

"That's too bad," the officer says. "I needed to talk to him about something important."

"I can't imagine what that might be," I continue, aware that I'm stammering slightly but unable to stop. "There's nothing you could possibly want with us."

"Is that right?" He pauses, with a slight frown. "Are you Mrs. Garrett?"

"I..." I take a deep breath. "I am," I say finally, feeling a flash of pride in my chest.

"I understand you and your husband live here with your daughter."

I nod, too scared to speak.

"Is she around right now?"

I shake my head.

"Are you okay, Mrs. Garrett?" he asks. "You seem kinda nervous."

"I'm fine," I blurt out, while cursing my inability to stay calm. "What do you *want*?"

"Well..." He pauses, as if he's thinking about something. "Well, to tell you the truth, we got reports that a salesman passing through the area earlier this week heard screams coming from somewhere around here. About Tuesday night?" He pauses yet again, still eying me with a hint of suspicion. "He said it sounded like a woman, sounded real bad too. He didn't get to town to report it until yesterday and, well, we thought we should look into it. From what he said, this house seems like the only likely place for it to have come from. We reckon anywhere else'd be too far off."

I wait for him to continue.

"Mrs. Garrett?" he says after a moment.

"What?" I ask, forcing a smile.

"Well... Did you or your family hear screams in this area on Tuesday night?"

I shake my head. He's talking about Mother's screams, of course, on her first night in the basement, but I can't possibly tell him that.

"Huh." He pauses again. "You didn't hear *anything*?"

I shake my head again.

"It's just," he continues, "the salesman said the screams were real loud, like... Well, it's hard to believe he could've heard them out there on the Montelbat road, but you folks here didn't hear a thing. I mean, he said he didn't think there were any houses out this way at all, but when he described the area, we realized there's this place so..." His voice trails off. "Well, M'am, it just seems a little odd, don't you think?"

"I don't know," I reply.

"You don't know?"

"I mean... I don't know what he heard, but I certainly didn't hear anything. Neither of us did."

"Neither of you?"

"I mean, none of us. We didn't hear a thing."

He opens his mouth to say something, but again he pauses. "You do seem *awfully* nervous, Mrs. Garrett. Are you sure there's nothing you want to tell me? Maybe while your husband's away from the property?"

I shake my head, while fighting the urge to burst into tears.

"Huh." He pauses again. "And when do you expect your husband back?"

"Later."

"Later?"

I nod.

"I see. Well..." He looks around for a moment, as if he's looking for something or someone. "Sorry," he continues, turning back to me, "just to be clear in my mind... You're *Mrs.* Garrett? Rebecca Garrett?"

I pause, before nodding.

"Okay. Sorry, it's just that you look quite..." Another pause. "And your daughter, that would be Annie Garrett, I believe?"

"She's out."

"I see. Out where?"

"With her father. It's perfectly natural. I mean, it's normal. I mean..."

My voice trails off, and I can't help thinking that it's better if I say as little as possible.

"Funny, really," he continues, taking off his hat and scratching the top of his head. "What with her being named Annie, and all."

"Why is that funny?" I ask.

"Well, it's just... What with the other Annie who drowned all those years back." He sighs, before setting his hat back on his head and turning back to go to his car. "Well, I'll be -"

"What other Annie?" I ask, taking a step toward him. "Who drowned?"

He turns to me, before looking toward the trees and pointing. "You don't know about Annie Shaw? There was a family who lived in this house about fifty years ago, before your husband's family moved here. Anyway, from what I hear, the previous owners had one child, a little girl named Annie, same name as your daughter, Mrs. Garrett." He pauses, watching the trees for a moment. "Little Annie drowned one summer, just disappeared in the middle of the lake. They say the family was so distraught, the father ended up drinking himself to death and the mother moved away. Such a tragic story."

"There was another girl named Annie here?" I ask, shivering a little at the suggestion. "How..."

For a moment, I think back to that day when I saw a face staring up at me from the depths of the lake. I'd written that moment off as some kind of trick of the light, but now...

"Well I'm sorry I disturbed you folks," he says finally, heading back to his car. "I just thought you'd most likely have heard something, but if you didn't, you didn't." He opens the door before turning to me. "Please tell your husband and daughter that I called by, and let them know that if they heard anything at all, they should get in touch with me at the Dunceford police station.

Now that's very important, you understand? If they heard *anything*, even if it didn't seem like something important, they need to let us know, even though..." He pauses, looking around. "Well, it's probably nothing."

I nod.

He dips his hat at me. "Well, M'am, good day to you."

I watch as he gets into his car and starts the engine. Frozen to the spot, I feel as if I can't move a muscle as his car pulls away and heads back along the dirt road. Even after he's out of sight beyond the line of trees in the distance, I stay standing, feeling a sense of cold dread creeping up my arms and across my shoulders. I can't even remember the last time I had to speak to someone from the town, and I'm not entirely sure that I allayed all of his concerns. Still, I'm sure he'll keep away; after all, I told him that we didn't hear any screams, and he has no reason to think me a liar. I sit back down to finish the potatoes, but my hands are trembling and I feel as if I'll cut myself if I continue, so I simply take a deep breath and wait for the fear to pass. The police officer won't be back, I know he won't. Why would he?

After a moment, I look toward the trees, and it's not hard to imagine a little girl staring back at me. Another Annie, a girl with the same name as me. As another shudder passes through my body, I get back to work.

CHAPTER SEVENTEEN

Today

IT'S LATE AND THE room is dark by the time I hear footsteps on the stairs again. I've spent the past few minutes staring out the window, watching the line of trees at the far end of the lawn; I look out every night like this, just soaking in the sense of emptiness and isolation while wondering about the little nudge in my chest, the hint that makes me think something might be staring back at me. Of course, tonight this is a way to distract myself from everything else that's going on, namely: why is my father suddenly such an asshole?

Still, it can't last much longer.

Mom'll put him in his place.

She has to. There's no way she's some kind of doormat.

A moment later, there's a creak on the floorboards outside my room, and a second after that the door starts to inch open, casting a shaft of light that slowly crosses my bed.

I already know who it is.

"I brought you some food," Dad says calmly.

I wait as he comes over to the bed and sets a plate on my bedside table. I know he's looking at me, but I don't want to dignify him by even looking at his miserable face right now. I honestly think I'd throw up, so instead I keep looking out the window, watching the distant trees.

"You know," he continues, "I expected your brother to act like a child. After all, he *is* a child. But you?" He waits for me to say something. "You're old enough to know better, Annie. You shouldn't sulk, it's a very immature way of dealing with things."

"So's locking someone in a basement," I reply through gritted teeth. "Did you let her out yet?"

"I'm going to do that soon."

I feel more anger bubbling through my body. I swear, if I could use my legs, I'd get out of this bed, storm downstairs, and start setting everything right. In my entire life, I've never felt so helpless.

"Scott ate his dinner," Dad says after a moment.

"Great."

"I hope you'll eat yours too."

"I'm not hungry."

"Annie -"

I turn to him, although the sight of his calm face immediately makes me want to wretch. "At what point in your life," I continue, "did you decide it's okay to start locking Mom in the goddamn basement?"

He sighs. "I was worried your mother's irrational fears would start to rub off on you and your brother. And, to be fair, that's exactly what has happened. Started to happen, anyway. I'm going to set that right."

"So you think this house is perfectly normal?"

"Come on, Annie, you've always been more like me, you know all that paranormal garbage is just... It's dumb. It's the kind of thing people like your mother believe so they can pretend there's something more to the world." He reaches down to touch the side of his face, but I pull away. "I've always felt that you're smarter than all of this garbage, Annie. Honestly, I had you pegged as an intelligent, rational young woman." He waits for a reply. "I hope you're not going to prove me wrong."

I take a deep breath, trying to keep from bursting into tears.

"With all due respect," he continues, "you have no idea what's really going on in this house. Sitting up here in bed, you must have ended up with a very warped perspective. You don't know what it's been like down there in the rest of the house over the past few days, your mother has... Well, let's just say that she's been acting very strangely. I even considered calling a doctor out, but I decided against it. We can handle all of this within the family, we don't need outsiders interfering."

"Outsiders?" I pause for a moment, staring at him. "That doesn't sound like something you'd say, Dad."

"You don't understand. You've been up here all the time."

"You make it sound like I had a choice," I mutter bitterly, through gritted teeth.

"Please don't start believing in the kind of thing your mother -"

"I believe in what I see," I reply, interrupting him. "Things that happen right in front of me, that's what I believe in and..." Feeling as if I'm being watched, I turn and glance at the open door. The brightly-lit landing *looks* bare, but at the same time I can't shake the feeling that something or someone is out there. After a moment, I see that light is catching the edges of something on the door-frame, and I realize it's picking out the words 'Annie's room' carved into the wood. "This isn't a good house," I continue. "You said you didn't want Mom to know about what happened here, but she's picked up on it all by herself."

"Nonsense."

"Then how do you -"

"She obviously read something," he replies. "Maybe she found the pages you'd been reading using her phone. Either that, or you disobeyed me and told her."

"Disobeyed you? What is this, the nineteenth century?"

"Don't be smart with me, young lady."

"Young lady? Since when did you start calling me *that*?"

"I can't talk to you right now," he replies, turning and heading across the room. He stops in the dark corner for a moment, and then he starts to wheel my chair out onto the landing.

"What are you doing?" I ask, sitting up.

"We don't want you getting any dumb ideas again, do we?" he says, stepping back in and taking my crutches too. "You've already tried to get up without permission once."

"Permission? What am I, a prisoner?"

"Of course not, but you're a child and you're stubborn." He stops in the doorway, watching me for a moment. "I expected this kind of irrational nonsense from your mother, and Scott's just a kid, but Annie... I really thought you were mature and smart enough to keep your head. I guess I was wrong about you."

"I guess I was wrong about you too," I tell him.

He pauses for a moment.

"I have to go and check on your mother," he says finally, before checking his watch. "It's getting late, you should eat your dinner and then sleep. With any luck everything'll be back to normal by breakfast and we can put this unpleasantness behind us. I hope you'll play your part in that process, Annie."

I watch in stunned silence as he closes the door.

"Can you at least leave that open?" I call out.

A moment later, I hear him wheeling the chair away.

"Are you serious?" I shout, listening to the sound of him heading downstairs. "What the hell is this, some kind of -"

Stopping suddenly, I realize I can see a shadow moving across the line of light at the bottom of the door, as if someone is out there on the landing. I wait, but after a moment I realize I can hear Dad talking to Scott down in the kitchen.

"Hello?" I say finally, trying not to sound scared. "Is someone there?"

The shadow loiters, but the door remains closed.

"I can see you," I continue. My heart is pounding in my chest and I feel as if every muscle in my body is tensing up. "What do you want?"

I wait.

The shadow remains for a few more seconds, before slipping away.

"Hey!" I call out, but it's too late. I sit and watch the door for a few more minutes, just in case there's any further sign of someone out there, and then I settle back on the bed. After a moment I reach out and switch on the nightlight. The room is bare and empty, but I can't shake the feeling that someone is nearby.

It must be Annie Garrett. After all, I'm in her room.

CHAPTER EIGHTEEN

Seventy-one years ago

"NO!" I SCREAM AS two of the officers manhandle me through the door and out onto the porch. "Stop! You can't do this!"

"Mrs. Garrett, please -"

"Stop!"

"Get her to the car," one of the other officers says. "She's getting hysterical."

"No!" Lashing out, I slam my elbow into the first officer's face and slip free, before two others grab me and pull me back. I reach out toward Father, who's sitting calmly and quietly at the kitchen table as if he's just going to let this happen. "Tell them!" I scream. "Tell them we didn't do anything wrong!"

"Where's your daughter?" one of the officers asks Father for the hundredth time since they all arrived a few minutes ago. "Mr. Garrett, where's Annie?"

Father doesn't reply. He simply stares at me with a hint of dread in his eyes.

"You have to leave!" I shout at the officers as tears roll down my cheeks. "You have no right to be here! This is private property!"

"We have every right, M'am," the first officer says, turning to me. "We're investigating reports of a scream out this way last week, and so far you two can't account for the disappearance of your daughter Annie Garrett. Now, we don't have any photos to help us, but we have census records and there should be a girl named Annie Garrett living at this property. This is your last chance to tell us where she is before you're both taken to the station for questioning."

"I -" Pausing, filled with rage as the officers hold me in the doorway, I realize I can't possibly tell the truth. I turn and watch as more officers continue to search the property. They'll never find Mother's grave, Father buried her body too deep, but still I resent the fact that they're here at all. We're quiet people and we keep to ourselves, and we deserve to be left alone instead of being harassed by a bunch of thugs who'd never be able to understand that we *needed* to kill Mother.

"Mrs. Garrett?" the officer says after a moment. "Do you have anything to say about Annie?"

I turn to him, and all of a sudden the tears seem to dry in my eyes. "No," I tell him finally. "I have nothing to say about Annie."

***

"Where's Annie Garrett?" the officer asks a few hours later, as we sit in an interview room at the police station. "Come on, you have to tell me. I know something happened to her. She's dead, isn't she?"

Staring back at him, I feel nothing but hatred for the fact that this pathetic, pig-like man thinks he has the right to hold me here and ask my questions. I want to reach across the table and wring his neck, but I know that'd only get me into trouble. Far better to let him do his thing until he gets tired, and then he'll have to let Father and I go.

"We found blood-stained clothes," he continues. "There were two dresses in bags in the basement, and there was more blood down there. We also found some more clothes dumped in the forest near the house." He waits for an answer. "Someone clearly lost a lot of blood at that property, and since your daughter Annie is missing -"

I let out a brief, impromptu laugh.

"Is something funny?" he asks.

I shake my head, quickly getting myself under control.

"Where's Annie?" he continues.

"I..." Taking a deep breath, I try to think of a way to make him understand. I look over at the door and think of Father, most likely in one of the other interview rooms. I know he won't tell them anything, so I just have to stay strong and we'll be out of here before sundown.

"I don't think you understand the seriousness of the situation," the officer continues. "I *can* charge both you and your husband with murder, even if we don't find

Annie's body. It'll look very bad for you if you go to trial and still don't say anything, there's no way that'll play well with a jury. Folks round here, they don't much like people who murder their children." He pauses. "I'm sure I don't need to remind you that we have the death penalty in this state, and women have been sent to the chair before."

Taking a deep breath, I force myself to remain calm.

"You look very good for your age," he says suddenly.

"I beg your pardon?"

He glances down at some papers. "Says here, Rebecca Garrett is thirty-two years old. I guess all that country living must be real good for the complexion."

"I don't see that my complexion is any of your business," I tell him.

"And your daughter Annie is sixteen," he continues, looking at me for a moment with just the faintest hint of suspicion. For a few seconds, it's almost as if he might suspect the truth. "Where *is* Annie, Mrs. Garrett? If your husband killed her, you can -"

"My husband didn't kill her," I snap back at him. "That's a preposterous idea, he loves her. He loves Annie more than any of you men could ever understand, and in a *way* that you couldn't understand."

"Is that so?"

"Most assuredly. He loves Annie purely, and wholly, and in a way that will never be broken." Feeling a surge of strength, I realize that this pathetic police officer can never break me. "He loves Annie with all of his heart," I continue, on the verge of tears, "and she loves him back from the very depths of her soul. Please, you can't possibly hope to understand such a powerful love. You must simply accept that it's true, and move on from your investigation. There is nothing for you to do here, nothing you can -"

"Mrs. Garrett -"

"You're meddling," I continue, unable to hold my anger back for a moment longer. "You don't understand love, not real love, not the true love that exists between my -" I catch myself just in time, before I admit the truth. "Do what you want," I add, trying once again to stay calm, "but you'll be fumbling about in the dark because I absolutely promise you, you're dealing with a type of love that is beyond your comprehension. You might as well ask me the rest of your questions in a foreign language, for all the good they'll do you. The last thing I'm willing to say, is that Annie Garrett is not dead. She's alive and well and happy, and no, I won't help you to find her. You never will." I pause. "You couldn't find her," I add finally, with a faint smile, "even if she was right in front of you."

He stares at me for a moment, clearly shocked, before clearing his throat.

"Until I see Annie with my own eyes," he says finally, "I can't take your word for any of that. And if I *don't* see her with my own eyes, then there's a very, very strong chance that you and your husband will be charged with her murder, and convicted of her murder, and sentenced to death for her murder. And that sentence will be carried out by means of either lethal injection or the electric chair." He pauses, staring at me. "Now, I don't want to see that happen, so I'll ask you again, Mrs. Garrett, and I sincerely hope you'll answer me this time. Where is Annie?"

I stare back at him. There's no point saying anything else. He'll never understand. Besides, he claims to be searching for Annie, yet I'm sitting right here in front of him. The man is clearly an imbecile.

"Alright, then," he mutters, getting to his feet. "I think I'm just going to go talk to my colleagues for a moment."

Left alone in the room, I sit completely still and stare at the opposite wall. I'm sure the police officers are feverishly discussing this case out in the corridor, but they'll never get to the truth because they'll never understand the kind of love Father and I have for one another. They won't find Mother's body, either. For the rest of it all, let them do what they want. They'll never understand the truth, and they'll never change any of it. I would rather die than do anything to jeopardize what I have with Father, and I'm certain he feels the same.

I'll stay quiet now. Father will be so proud of me.

CHAPTER NINETEEN

Today

"HEY!" I SHOUT, LOUDER than before. "Can someone please come and tell me what the hell is going on?"

I wait, sitting up in bed, propped against the wall. It's around eight or nine in the morning and sunlight is streaming through the window. After a restless night that brought little sleep, I feel exhausted but edgy, and I'm starting to wonder just when someone is going to come up and see me. Mom would usually have come by now, just to check on me, but there's been no sign of her. In fact, despite a few bumps during the night, the house has been suspiciously quiet since Dad left me in here a little over twelve hours ago. The door has remained shut and I don't hear anyone moving about downstairs. I'm not going to panic, not yet, but still...

"Dad!" I shout. "Mom! Can one of you guys

come up?"

"I wait.

"Please?"

Silence.

I stare at the door, waiting in vain for some hint of movement out there. It's Tuesday today, and Mom at least is usually up around dawn since we arrived in the new house. Sure, it's possible that they've all decided to sleep in, but they must be able to hear me calling out to them and Scott, at least, should have come to tell me I need to be quiet. Leaning across the bed, I glance out the window, but the car is still down in the driveway. I guess they might have all gone out very early, maybe to explore the forest, but it's odd that they didn't let me know first. Maybe I was asleep, but I can't shake the feeling, deep down, that something might be wrong.

"This isn't funny," I mutter, leaning back and forcing myself to stay calm. "What am I supposed to do, just sit in my room forever?"

***

Looking up from my book, I glance at the door as I realize I just heard a very faint creaking sound out there.

"Hello?" I say cautiously.

No reply.

"Dad?"

I wait.

"If this is some kind of punishment," I continue, "it's completely lame. You realize that, right?"

Silence.

It's midday and I've spent the morning reading. I ate last night's dinner for breakfast, which was cold and unpleasant, but I've managed to quell my sense of panic by telling myself that Mom and Dad must have taken Scott out to explore the land surrounding the house. They sort of, kind of mentioned doing something like that a few times, and although I'm a little annoyed that they'd leave me here alone like this, I figure I must have been asleep when they set off, and they probably didn't want to wake me. Maybe Mom persuaded Dad to go out with her so they could try to clear the air.

I mean, that's the only possible explanation.

I wait a moment longer, in case there's another sound from the landing, but after a few seconds I start to realize that the house is completely quiet. We're so far from civilization, there's not even any kind of sound outside, just the occasional cry of a bird. I lean over and look outside again, hoping to -

Suddenly I see her.

It's the woman from before, wearing a white dress and with her back to me, and she's standing more or less where I saw her the first time.

I watch her for a moment, before reaching out and tapping on the window.

No reply.

With a little pain, I pull myself across the bed until I'm closer to the window, and then I tap on the glass again.

"Hey!" I shout, hoping she'll be able to hear me.

She doesn't react at all.

Setting my book aside, I reach across the bedside

table and start fumbling with the latch. It's not easy, but finally I get the damn thing open and I start to slide the window up. A cold breeze enters the room, causing me to shiver a little, and I watch the woman for a moment, feeling as if maybe I shouldn't disturb her. Then again, she's on my family's property and as far as I can tell, she has no permission to be anywhere near the house. I hesitate for a moment, before figuring that I should at least try to get her attention.

"Hey!" I call out. "Are you okay there? Do you want something?"

I wait, but still she doesn't respond at all. This time, with the window open, I know she must be able to hear me. The cool breeze is rippling her dress, and the distant trees are swaying slightly, but the woman herself seems lost in her own thoughts.

"Can I help you?" I shout, before banging my fist on the window-ledge in an attempt to get her attention. "Hey! You there, can you -"

Suddenly she turns to me, and I freeze as I see the pained look on her face. I was expecting someone young, and in the back of my mind I was even wondering if she might be Annie Garrett, but it's immediately clear that this is an older woman, in her thirties at least. She's still a good fifteen meters away, but when I squint I can just about make out her features, and her eyes in particular are striking, with dark, heavy-looking rings. The way she's staring at me, it's as if there's great sorrow in her soul, but also a hint of anger.

And then she turns, and then she starts slowly walking toward the house.

Step by step, she comes closer, making for the porch.

"Hey!" I call out. "What do you want?"

She doesn't reply. Her gaze is fixed on the house now, on the door that's directly below my room, leading into the kitchen.

"Maybe you can come back later," I tell her, bristling a little as I realize that she's already halfway across the lawn now. "My parents will be back soon."

She doesn't look up at me. She just keeps walking until she reaches the steps that lead up onto the porch.

"Hey! Stop!"

Craning my neck, I look down and see her disappear from view beneath the porch's wooden roof. I wait for her to knock on the door, but as the seconds pass I realize that I can't hear her at all and the sound of her footsteps has stopped. I keep telling myself that it's okay, that I definitely didn't hear the back door opening; at the same time, I can't shake the fear that maybe the door was already open, and that the woman has silently entered the house.

"Hello?" I call out.

I wait.

No reply.

"Are you down there?" I wait again. "You can't come in, you'll have to wait 'til someone's around. Sorry, I'm -"

Hearing a bump, I turn and look toward my closed bedroom door. The sound was so brief and so weak, I can't even be sure it was really there.

I hold my breath.

Silence.

I want to call out again, but at the same time I don't want to draw any more attention to myself. Turning, I look back out the window, but the lawn is bare now. Glancing toward the trees, I realize that my family are probably out there somewhere, having a great time and just assuming I'm fine here alone. I look down at the porch's roof and try to imagine the woman still standing there; after all, I'd have seen her if she'd left, and I refuse to believe that she came into the house, so she *must* be on the porch still.

Maybe she's waiting.

For what?

"Hello?" I call out again, my voice faltering slightly. "Can you... If you're there, can you say something?"

No reply.

The only sound comes from the wind as it ruffles the distant trees.

Leaning back, I sit in silence for a few minutes, desperately alert in case there's any hint of movement in the house. I keep expecting to hear a creaking sound or a bump, but gradually I start to relax just a little. I try to run through the possibilities, and more than anything I want to start believing that the woman wasn't really there, or that she managed to slip away and now she's long gone. After all, I don't really know what the porch is like, so I guess there could be a way for her to have left without being seen. Staring at my door, however, I start imagining the possibility that she's downstairs now, or that she's coming up.

I wait.

"Mom!" I call out. "Dad! Scott! If one of you is here, now would be a *really* good time to drop in and check on me, okay?"

Silence.

"Guys?"

No answer.

Although I want to go back to reading my book, I can't stop staring at the door. It's a long-shot, but *if* that woman came into the house, I have to be ready for her. I mean, for all I know, she might be some kind of escaped lunatic from a nearby asylum, or a crazy neighbor who has no idea about personal boundaries. My heart is pounding but I tell myself that I'm overreacting, that there's a rational explanation even though I can't figure it out just yet. After all, stuck here in my room with no real idea of the house's layout, I don't have the best perspective, so I figure I just have to be patient.

All the while, the silent house seems to be closing in around me.

***

I flick the switch and my bedside light blinks to life. Well, at least there's still power.

It's getting dark outside now. All afternoon, I've tried to read my book while spending long stretches just staring at the door. The last thing I want to do is start panicking, and besides, it's not like I can get up and start looking around. I've managed to convince myself that my initial assessment must be true: Mom, Dad and Scott went out to spend the day exploring our new surroundings, and they'll be home for dinner. Hell, they might even have found somewhere to hang out and enjoy a picnic. I mean, I'd be mad at them for leaving me alone like this, but I'd also be very, *very* relieved to see them coming home.

Turning to look out the window, I see that the dark forest looks darker now, while the cold evening sky is folding blue as night starts to fall. For a moment, I think I can see a figure out there, hiding between the trees, but it's gone when I blink. Must have been a trick of the light.

I check my watch and see that it's a little after 6pm. The others should be home soon. They *have* to be home soon.

They wouldn't just leave me alone all day without any food.

Picking up the book, I try once again to distract myself by reading, but again my gaze shifts to the bedroom door. There are no lights on the landing, so this time all I see under the door is a line of darkness. It has been five or six hours since I saw the woman on the lawn, but mercifully there's been no hint that she's inside the house, not even so much as an unexplained creaking sound. I haven't seen her leave, either, but I guess I don't really know what the house is like on the outside, so she probably just slipped away without being noticed.

I'll laugh about all of this tomorrow. That's what I keep telling myself.

After reading the same paragraph over and over

again, and still not taking any of it in, I set the book down and wait for a moment.

I start counting.

One.

Two.

Damn it, I can't take this anymore.

"Hey!" I shout, just in case the others got home and I didn't hear them. "Is someone going to actually come up here?"

Silence.

"Great," I mutter, leaning back and still watching the door. I'm going to give them hell for this when they get back. They *will* get back, though. I mean, they have to come home soon.

***

"Come on!" I shout, lifting the bedside table and letting its legs bang on the wooden floor again. "You guys! Seriously, what the hell is going on around here?"

It's late now, almost 9pm, and I'm starting to get really worried. All my earlier explanations, all my theories about them going out to explore the area, are starting to fall apart. There's just no way they'd leave me alone to fend for myself for so long, especially without letting me know first. Even if I was asleep and they didn't want to wake me, they could have left a note and brought some food up. Instead, I've been making do with a solitary glass of water and a few pickings from the dinner Dad brought up for me last night, but that was almost twenty-four hours ago and now I'm hungry and thirsty.

With tears in my eyes, I look out the window again, but there's only darkness.

I switch off the bedside lamp, to better see the view. Far beyond the empty lawn, the line of trees has become a thick, dark shape and it's getting harder and harder to believe that the others are out there somewhere. Figuring that I don't want to be left without light, I switch the lamp back on and turn to look at the door again, and then I settle down on the bed and stare at the ceiling. There are still tears in my eyes, and although the last thing I want is to start crying like some kind of baby, I'm starting to feel seriously worried and alone.

All I can do is tell myself that my parents and Scott will be back soon.

Then they'll explain where they went.

Then we'll work out who the woman was.

And then everything will be okay.

I wait.

Silence.

And then a click, from somewhere nearby. It only lasts for half a second or so, but I immediately know what it is. Slowly, I turn and look across the room.

My bedroom door is opening.

Slowly.

So slowly, I didn't even think a door *could* open that slowly.

As it creaks open, the door reveals the dark landing on the other side.

Holding my breath, I wait as the door continues to swing open. I'm convinced there's going to be someone out there, someone looking in at me, but a few seconds later the door is open wide enough for me to see that there's no-one.

Finally, the door bumps against the dresser. Open all the way now, the empty doorway seems to be staring in at me.

I don't move.

I don't dare.

Listening to the silence, I keep expecting to hear another creak on the floorboards. Although I try to tell myself that Scott is pulling a prank on me, or that the door opened of its own accord even though it was properly shut a moment ago, deep down I know that it's neither of those things.

I wait.

And wait.

And wait, until I start to feel as if something else is waiting for *me*.

"Hello?" I say finally, keeping my voice low. I sound terrified, but there's a good reason for that: I *am* terrified. "Hello?" I say again, a little more loudly this time, as I sit up in bed. I want to sound confident, not afraid, in case someone's listening, but it's not easy.

Silence.

And then, slowly, a creak from one of the floorboards on the landing.

Someone's out there.

"Mom?" I call out, no longer able to hide the emotion from my voice. I'm too scared to cry, but I can't help gripping the bedsheets and pulling myself along until my back is against the wall. "Dad? Scott? Are you out there? Please, if you are, just let me know."

The empty doorway continues to stare at me.

"Who is it?" I ask, even though I'm terrified of receiving an answer.

Nothing.

"What do you want?"

I'm getting desperate now, but I know I have to stay calm. I look down at my plaster-clad legs and realize that there's still no way I can walk. If Dad had left the wheelchair or the crutches in here, I might have had a chance, but right now my only option is to get down and drag myself across the floor. I'm not sure I'm ready to do that, though; I don't want to admit that something's seriously wrong, not yet.

"Is anyone here?" I call out, my voice cracking with fear. "Please, if you're here, I don't want any trouble. If you just tell me what you want, maybe I can help you."

I wait.

"Please?" I whisper, swallowing hard.

I sit in silence, waiting for something, anything to happen, but I'm starting to feel more and more as if something's out there waiting for me. I keep clinging to the hope that this is all a huge misunderstanding, but I'm also starting to think that maybe there's been some kind of accident. If Mom, Dad and Scott went out into the forest, they might have got hurt and now no-one's coming to help me, or worse still, maybe someone hurt them and now that person is here.

There's one other thing I want to call out, but I'm worried about what might happen. Then again, I have no choice.

"Annie?" I say finally, staring at the empty doorway. "Annie Garrett, are you there?"

Silence.

Taking a deep breath, I try to stay calm. One thing's certain: I can't just sit here forever, waiting to learn the truth.

I have to do something.

Scooching over to the edge of the bed, I look down at the bare floorboards. This whole idea feels crazy, but at the same time I have no other options left. I turn a little and then lean down, propping myself on my elbow before inching away from the bed, making sure to bump my legs as little as possible. It's not exactly a graceful endeavor, but I have no choice. Once my hips are clear, I start to lower myself down and then I roll onto my back and use my elbows to inch toward the wall, while letting my legs slide down as slowly as possible. Finally I lean forward and grab my right thigh, and then I carefully move my leg down so that it's resting on the floor. I do the same with the other leg and, after a few more awkward grunts and twists I'm out of bed and flat on my back.

A little out of breath, I turn and look at the door.

It's still open.

Still waiting.

After carefully rolling onto my front, I prop myself on my elbows again and start to make my way forward, wriggling like some kind of ungainly worm. My legs, packed tight in the plaster casts, are heavy as they drag behind me, but fortunately there's not much pain, just a hint of discomfort. I reach the doorway and look up. On the frame, the words 'Annie's room' are clearly visible scratched into the wood. I have no idea what to do, but I figure there's no turning back now so I inch forward and lean through to the landing.

Looking both ways, I realize that the whole house, apart from my room, is in darkness. I can see a light-switch over on the far wall, but there's no way I can reach up there. I was hoping to spot my crutches somewhere nearby, or the wheelchair, but Dad must have moved them further away. There's still no sign of anyone, and while the area immediately outside my bedroom door is bathed in a little low light, the other rooms are dark and I can barely make out the top of the stairs at the far end of the corridor.

Still using my elbows, I crawl out onto the landing and make my way over to the nearest door, which I think leads into Mom and Dad's room. It's closed, of course, so I knock hard and wait for someone to answer, before realizing that I need to get inside. Propping myself up with my left elbow, I reach for the handle and manage to get a few fingertips onto the side; after a couple of attempts, I'm just about able to turn the handle and get the door to click open, and then I push it all the way and look through into the dark bedroom.

"Hello?" I call out, hoping against hope that Mom and Dad will turn out to have been in bed all along.

I wait.

Nothing.

Craning my neck, I can see that the bed is neat

and made. I look around, squinting in the darkness as I see various unopened packing crates, but there's clearly no-one in here.

"Mom?" I shout. "Dad? Can you hear me?"

I bang my fist against the floor, hoping to attract a little attention, but of course no-one comes. I feel like there's a knot of panic in my chest, and with each passing second the knot is twisting tighter and tighter.

"Great," I mutter, backing out of the room awkwardly until I'm on the landing again. My first instinct is to head to the stairs, but I figure I should check Scott's room so I crawl along, already feeling tired in my arms. When I get to the door, I reach up and turn the handle, and after pushing the door open I'm able to see through into the darkness. Scott's room, like all the others, has barely been decorated since we arrived, although I can see his bed that we brought from the old house. There's no sign of him, but the air smells musty and after a moment I realize that the smell is vaguely familiar. Against my better judgment, I crawl over to his bed and sit up, and sure enough the smell is stronger here.

There's a dark, wet patch on the sheets. It's been year since Scott last peed the bed, but there's no doubting what happened in here.

Turning, I start crawling back toward the door. Once I'm out on the landing, I make my way to the top of the stairs and look down, but there's no light and no hint of movement from below. The house is clearly empty.

"Hello?" I shout, even though I know they'd

have been able to hear me long before now if they were around. "Mom? Dad? Please, can you just..."

I hold my breath, before letting out a gasp of frustration. There are tears in my eyes again, but I'm determined not to cry. Instead, I focus on how the hell I'm going to get down these stairs, since they're steep and there's no carpet to help cushion my journey. Figuring that my best bet is to use the railings and go head first, I reach out and make sure to get a good grip. If I slip and fall, I could end up badly hurt or worse, but at the same time I have no choice, I have to get downstairs and then maybe I can find a phone and call for help. Even if Mom and Dad come back with a reasonable explanation, I think I'm well within my rights to be freaking out by now.

Taking care to move slowly, I inch forward over the top of the stairs and start lowering myself down. I work carefully and methodically, going down one step at a time despite the growing pain in my arms. Once my waist is over the edge, I have to take even more care, since the last thing I need is to knock my damaged legs. The whole process is achingly slow, and around the halfway point I start wondering whether I've made a mistake; still, I keep going and it must be at least ten minutes before I manage to get all the way down. I let out a sigh of relief as I stop and take a brief rest in the hallway, with the light of the moon shining through the glass panel and at least allowing me to see my immediate surroundings.

Even down here, Mom and Dad haven't really done any decorating. A few familiar pieces of furniture from the old house are dotted around, but the place feels very alien still and very uncomfortable.

It take a moment for me to turn around, but I manage to crawl through the nearest doorway, finding myself at the foot of a table with several wooden chairs around the sides. I glance past the table and see the kitchen, which means I'm directly beneath my bedroom. Crawling around the table, I let out a gasp of pain as I realize my elbows are starting to get sore, but I keep going until I reach the middle of the room, at which point I stop again and look around. There are a few items on the counter, and the dishwasher has been left open with a clean load still waiting to be taken out. That, in itself, strikes me as odd, since unloading the dishwasher has been Scott's job since time immemorial.

It's as if everything in the house just stopped.

"Hello!" I shout, looking around the room. "Is -"

I stop suddenly as I see that the porch door has been left open, allowing a cool draft to blow into the house. Thinking back to the woman I saw on the lawn earlier, I realize that since the door is open, she *could* have entered the house without making a noise. I turn and look over my shoulder, back toward the hallway, but there's still no sign of anyone. Hell, if there *is* another soul in the house, then they certainly know that *I'm* here. I start to crawl forward, making my way past the stove until I reach another door and look through into what turns out to be the front room. There are packing boxes everywhere, which strikes me as odd since I'd have thought Mom and Dad would have at least got everything in place by now. After all, it's been five days since I arrived home, and Mom said they were working hard.

Outside, a light rain has started to fall in the darkness, tapping against the windows.

Suddenly I hear footsteps.

Turning, I look around frantically, and then as if from nowhere a figure walks past the door at the other end of the kitchen, straight across the hallway. Almost as soon as I see it, it's gone again. In the dark, I can't make out any of the figure's features, but it was definitely a woman and I'm certain it wasn't Mom.

I freeze, but the sound of footsteps is gone now.

Opening my mouth, I'm about to call out when I realize that whoever it is, they must know I'm here by now. I turn and look the other way, toward the door that leads down to the basement.

I wait.

The only sound comes from the window, where more rain is falling.

Crawling forward as quickly as I can manage, I ignore the pain in my elbows and make my way past the sofa. After a moment, however, I let out a gasp of pain as I catch my right leg on the sofa's trailing edge, and I have to stop for a few seconds as the pain throbs and then fades. Although I'm trying to not make any noise, I can't keep my breathing under control and I feel certain that anyone else in the house can hear me. I look around, hoping against hope that I might spot something I can use as a weapon, but finally I realize my only chance is to get out of here and try to find help. Turning, I crawl back through to the kitchen, heading for the porch door while glancing over my shoulder to make sure that there's no sign of -

Suddenly I hear a sobbing sound nearby. I turn again, and to my stunned relief I see that Scott is in the corner, next to the open door. He's crying while sitting with his knees drawn up toward his face, and his whole body is shaking, but at least it's him!

"Scott!" I hiss, crawling over and immediately putting my arms around him, giving him a huge, tight hug. After a moment, I pull back. "What the hell's going on here, where are Mom and Dad?"

His eyes dart in my direction, but tears are streaming down his face and he makes no attempt to answer me.

"Scott," I whisper, reaching out and putting a hand on his shoulder to make sure that he's real, "what's wrong? Scott, you have to -"

Smelling something familiar, I look down and see that he's soiled himself again. There's a patch of urine on the floorboards, but he's made no attempt to move and his pants are soaked.

"Scott," I continue, "you have to listen to me. We need to get out of here and find Mom and Dad, do you understand? We need to get help."

He stares at me for a moment, his bottom lip trembling as if he's on the verge of saying something. It's almost as if something has broken him, and when I look into his eyes I see pain and fear staring back at me.

"Scott, I can't do this without you." I wait for him to reply, but a moment later he turns and looks past me, and I can immediately tell from his shocked expression that he's seen something.

Turning, I see that the figure from before is walking out of the room, quickly disappearing into the hallway.

"Did you see that too?" I ask, turning back to Scott. "Where have you guys been all day?"

"Here," he stammers, his voice choked with tears.

"Here?" I stare at him. "You've been right here all day, like this?"

"I..." He stares at me, but he's shaking too much to say anything.

"Did you hear me calling out?" I ask. "I was in my room, I was trying to get someone's attention."

"I couldn't do anything," he sobs. "I heard you, but I couldn't move."

"Did you -"

Before I can finish, there's a loud bumping sound from one of the upstairs rooms. Someone's definitely up there.

"Where are Mom and Dad?" I ask, turning back to Scott. When he doesn't answer, I crawl closer and put my hands on his shoulders. "Scott, I know you're scared but right now you have to listen to me, okay? I need to know where Mom and Dad are, and I need to -"

"She's coming," he replies, his voice sounding a little firmer this time.

"Who's coming?" I ask.

No reply.

"Scott," I continue, "*who's* coming? Is it Mom? Is Mom coming?"

He shakes his head.

"Then who?" I ask.

He opens his mouth, but the tears are running more freely than ever.

"Who's coming?" I continue, trying to stay calm. "Scott, tell me!"

"Annie," he whispers, his voice so tense with fear, it's as if he might shatter. He turns and looks out through the open porch door. "Annie's coming."

"Annie? Scott, *I'm* Annie, I'm right -"

I stop suddenly, before turning and looking out toward the lawn. In the distance, the line of trees can just about be made out in the darkness.

"Annie's coming," Scott says again. "The first Annie."

"The..." Figuring that he must mean Annie Garrett, I turn to him. "Have you seen her?"

He shakes his head. "She's coming."

"Scott," I continue, "I need you to work with me, okay? Just answer a couple of questions. Where's Mom?"

He stares at me, before looking down at the floor.

"Scott, answer me! Where is she?"

I wait, before suddenly realizing that by staring at the floor, maybe he *is* answering me.

"In the basement?" I ask. "Scott, is Mom in the basement?"

"Dad was really mad at her," he continues, sniffing back more tears. "He was so mad, he..."

I wait for him to continue.

"He what?" I ask finally, refusing to believe that Dad would ever do anything truly bad. "Scott, what did Dad do? Where's Mom now?"

"I don't know," he replies, breaking down into a fresh wave of sobs. "Dad had a shovel."

"It's okay," I tell him, putting an arm around his trembling shoulder. "Everything's going to be okay," I add, even though I know those words sound so hollow right now. Glancing back, I see the door to the basement and realize that I'm going to have to check to see if Mom's down there. "Scott," I continue, "I need you to do something, and it's really important, okay?"

I wait for him to reply, before pulling back and putting my hand under his chin. When I tilt his face up, I see his tear-stained face staring back at me.

"I need you to find the car keys," I tell him. "Do you know where Mom and Dad kept them? They used to put them in the fruit-bowl in the old apartment, remember? What about here? Where do they keep all the keys, do you know?"

He shakes his head.

"Then I need you to find them," I continue. "Look in coat pockets, in bowls, in drawers, anywhere you think they could be. Do you think you can do that?"

He glances past me, as if he's scared that he'll see the figure again.

"Don't think about any of that," I add. "Scott, no-one's going to come and help us, so we have to go and *get* help. Not just for us, but for Mom and Dad too. I'll check the basement, but you have to find the car keys, do you understand?"

He stares at me for a moment, before slowly nodding.

"Okay," I continue, using my elbows to turn around. "Meet me out front by the car, and don't worry. There's nothing here that can hurt you. Even if you think you see someone, it's just..." I pause for a moment, staring at the empty room and the doorway ahead. "It's just whispers of people, that's all. Whispers can't hurt us."

"But -"

"Just go!" I shout, as I start to crawl across toward the basement door. "Ignore everything else and find those keys!"

Glancing over my shoulder, I see to my relief that he's gotten to his feet and is looking on the kitchen counter. Turning, I crawl toward the basement door and when I look up I see to my relief that the padlock is hanging loose. I reach for the handle, but it's a little higher than the others and it takes a moment before I can get a few fingertips onto the edge. I have to try several times, but finally I get the damn thing to turn and manage to pull the door open. The effort is extreme, and I'm breathless by the time I manage to look down into the darkness below.

"Mom?" I shout. "Mom, are you down there?"

I wait, desperately hoping that she'll reply.

After a couple of seconds, I start to crawl forward, dropping down onto the top step. With just the kitchen's moonlit wall to help, I peer down into the darkness, but even squinting isn't enough and I can't see a damn thing. I wince with pain as I start to pull myself down a few more steps, until my hips drop onto the top step and I find that I can peer through the railings. I have no idea how large the basement is supposed to be, but I can't see anything at all. As my eyes adjust to the dark, I'm just about able to make out the brick wall extending away from the steps, but that doesn't help too much.

"Mom?" I call out, as tears start rolling down my face. "Mom, please, I need you. Please, you have to -"

Suddenly there's a loud bump, followed by another. I wait, frozen with fear, and to my horror I see a figure starting to make its way slowly up the steps toward me, emerging from the darkness of the basement. With a growing sense of horror, I realize that it's the woman from the lawn. She stops for a moment, her cold, dead eyes fixed on me, criss-crossed by what appear to be hundreds of little scratches; a fraction of a second later, she starts running up toward me, her feet banging on the steps as she reaches out.

"No!" I shout, instinctively pulling back and starting to haul myself back up through the doorway as she's about to grab me. Fumbling with the door, I manage to push it shut just in time to keep her from coming out. I look up at the handle, expecting it to turn, but there's nothing.

I wait.

My heart is pounding so fast, I feel as if it might burst out of my chest at any moment.

"Who are you?" I scream, leaning against the door in case she tries to get through. "What have you done with my parents?"

A moment later, I hear someone sobbing nearby.

I turn, but I don't see anyone. Still, the sobbing continues and I can't tell it's not Scott. It sounds like a woman, but it's coming from all around, as if someone's sorrow and grief is hanging in the air.

For a moment, I feel as if I can't go on. I'm exhausted and in pain, and I still don't understand what's going on here. After a couple of seconds, however, my strength returns and I realize that I have to go and find Scott. Grabbing a nearby wooden chair, I push it against the basement door and wedge the back under the handle. Turning, I start crawling across the floor, heading for the porch door in the hope that Scott has found the keys and has gone to wait for my by the car. Just as I'm about to reach the door, however, I hear a banging sound, and I turn just in time to see the chair flying through the air, smashing into the opposite wall. The basement door opens and the woman steps through, her damaged eyes fixed on me.

"Please," I whimper, with tears running down my face, "whatever you want..."

"You have to get out of here," she replies with a cold, terrified voice as she turns looks toward the back door. "She's coming."

"Who's coming?" I ask, although I think I already know the answer. "Is it Annie? Is Annie coming?"

I wait, before turning as I hear a bumping sound from the room above. A moment later, glancing toward the hallway, I spot something moving down the stairs. Footsteps. Slow, calm footsteps.

"Is that her?" I ask, using my elbows to crawl

past the woman and over to the porch door. "What does she want?"

"She wants you," the woman replies, turning to look down at me. "It might be too late."

"She wants me? What -"

"Run!" she screams, staring across the lawn. "Get away from her!"

Panicking, I turn and crawl out onto the porch and then over toward the steps. Light rain is still falling but all I can think about is that I have to get away from the house. I don't even stop when I reach the steps; instead, I throw myself down and try to stop my fall with my hands as I clatter toward the bottom. Landing hard, I let out a cry of pain as I feel my legs banging against the steps, but even *that* doesn't stop me. I gasp as I start to drag myself away, while looking around for some sign of Scott. I can see the car, but Scott's not with it so I look toward the trees. Figuring he must have gone that way, I start dragging myself across the lawn as rain falls all around.

Digging my hands into the rain-soaked mud, I start pulling myself along.

"Mom!" I scream. "Help me!"

I don't know how I manage to keep going with the pain in my arms and legs, but somehow I manage to drag my exhausted, broken body through the mud and rain for a few more meters before looking back over my shoulder. Sure enough, there's a figure in the doorway, stepping through and making its way down to join me on the lawn.

Annie Garrett.

It has to be her.

"Leave me alone!" I shout, with tears running down my cheeks. "What do you want from me?"

Turning again, I keep going, hauling myself across the lawn even though I know the figure must be catching up to me. All I can think about is that I have to get to safety and that I have to find Scott and make sure he's okay. Hopefully Mom was able to get away, and Dad too, and eventually we can figure out exactly what the hell happened in this place. I dig my hands deeper into the mud, struggling to get a grip, until I've pulled myself a little further along. This time, however, when I bury my fingers in the mud ready to drag myself again, I feel something hard against my fingertips. A moment later, I stare in horror as I lift a bare human skull out of the mud, its bony surface lit by the moonlight. There are flecks of mud on the skull's face, but rain is quickly washing it clean, and all I can do is stare in horror, even as a shadow falls across me from behind and I realize that the woman from the house is here.

"Annie," a voice whispers, sounding weak and frail. "Help me."

"What?" I stare at the skull as I realize that the voice seemed to come from its mouth. After a moment, I start to recognize the voice, although there's no way...

"Annie," it says again, "please..."

I blink, and suddenly I realize that the skull isn't a skull at all. It's my mother, with just her face poking out from the mud as if someone tried to bury her.

"Help me," she whispers, before looking past me. Her eyes widen in horror, and then she screams:

"Annie! Help!"

Frantically trying to dig her out from the muddy pit, I struggle until I'm able to get her arms free, which allows her to help herself. There's a thick, bloody wound on the side of her head, with fresh blood mixed with mud and running down onto her face. After a moment, I spot a shovel half-buried in the mud nearby.

"Where's Scott?" she stammers, wincing with pain.

"I don't know," I reply. "Where's Dad?"

"Your father..." She gasps as fresh blood flows from her wound. "Your father tried to kill me. He tried to bury me alive."

"No," I say firmly, "Dad wouldn't do that, Dad would never -"

"It wasn't really him," she stammers, before looking past me. "Annie..." She lets out a faint gasp, before losing consciousness.

"Mom!" I shout, trying to shake her back awake. "Mom, you have to listen to me! You have to -"

I freeze as I see a shadow falling across me from behind. Suddenly the dead woman crouches down next to us, and I turn to see that she's staring straight ahead, watching the trees at the far end of the lawn.

"She's coming," she says, her voice filled with terror. "I tried to help you, but now she's coming."

"Who's coming?" I ask, staring at her.

"Annie," she replies. "Annie's coming."

"But..." I pause for a moment. "You mean Annie Garrett? Is that who's coming?"

"No," she replies, Annie Garrett was my

daughter. She's gone, she was taken away but..." She pauses, and then she points toward the trees. "There. *She's* coming. The other Annie."

"Who?" I shout, as rain continues to fall. "Who are you talking about?"

"Annie Shaw," she replies. "The first Annie. She was there in the background all along, hiding. She's the one who turned *my* Annie into a monster. Now she's going to do the same thing to you."

"What are you talking about?" I ask. "You're -"

"There!" she shouts, pointing toward the forest. "She's here!"

Turning, I see to my horror that there's a figure just about visible in the darkness, emerging from between the trees. I watch for a moment as the figure limps slowly forward, making its way directly toward us.

"Who's that?" I whisper, feeling a growing sense of shock creeping through my chest. After a moment, I turn to the woman. "Who is it?" I shout. "Please, you have to tell me what's happening!"

"She's the first Annie," she replies. "She's the one who lived here even before any of us, the one who drowned in the lake. Ever since then..." She turns to me. "All she wants is a father. Someone she can love, and who'll love her in return. She never had a childhood, but they never found her body in the lake so her soul remained and she wants to experience the love of a family. She tried to use my daughter, but it all went wrong. Now she's going to try again with you."

I watch as the distant figure comes closer. As it limps into a patch of moonlight, I see to my horror that it's a girl, only nine or ten years old, her entire body rotten and putrid. Scraps of torn fabric hang from her skeletal frame, and her dead face has been stripped of almost all its flesh, leaving a stunted nose and two dark, hollow eyes.

"I'm sorry," the dead woman whispers. "I tried to warn you."

"No," I whisper, turning to see that my mother is still unconscious. "We have to get out of here," I tell her, grabbing her by the shoulder. "Mom, wake up! We have to find Dad and Scott and leave!"

Turning, I see that the dead girl is standing over us now, staring directly at me.

"My daughter tried to give her what she wanted," Annie Garrett's mother says calmly, "but she ended up as a bitter, twisted monster." She turns to me. "If you fight back, she'll do the same thing to you. Maybe it's better this way. Just give the little girl what she wants. Let her feel the love of a family through you. Don't fight it."

As the rotting girl reaches down toward me through the rain, all I can do is scream.

CHAPTER TWENTY

Seventy-one years ago

"REBECCA GARRETT," THE WARDEN says solemnly as he stands before me, "before the judgment of the court is carried out, is there anything you wish to say?"

Strapped into the chair, with thick restraints around my legs, wrists and neck, I stare at the imbecile. He's just like all the others. They managed to hold a full trial without ever realizing the truth; they think Annie Garrett is dead and buried somewhere, and they think I'm Mother. Father and I never told them the truth, of course. Father has barely spoken a word since the day the police turned up at the house, while I refuse to explain the situation. I would rather die like this, than cheapen the truth by whispering it into the ears of idiots.

"I'll take your silence as a refusal to speak," the warden continues. "It will be noted in the records that you waived your opportunity to make a statement."

As he turns and walks away, he doesn't see the little girl standing in the middle of the room. Dripping wet and rotten, she stares at me with dark eyes. I've seen her every day since Father and I were dragged from our home; the girl seems to be watching over me, as if she wants to witness my fate. I have no doubt that she is the first Annie, Annie Shaw, the little girl who once lived in our house and who drowned in the lake beyond the forest. Sometimes, when the world is quiet or when I'm close to sleep, I feel as if I can hear her voice whispering in my thoughts. In fact, looking back over the events of the past few years, I'm sure she must have been meddling, manipulating the situation and perhaps even changing the way we all behaved.

Did Father sense her too? Is that why he seemed so thoughtful all the time? Out there working so often, he must surely have realized that he was being watched by this little girl who wanted a family again.

On the far side of the room, the warden and his assistants are making ready to throw the switch and end my life. One of them has taken a black hood from a box, and now he's coming over to me.

"I'm sorry I couldn't give you what you wanted," I whisper, staring at the dead girl. "Perhaps we can be together again at the house. Perhaps someone else will move in, and she can give you a family?"

As soon as he reaches me, the man places the black hood over my head. I suppose these fools don't want to see my face as I die, but now I'm in darkness I feel quite certain that the little girl is still there, still watching from beyond the grave. I never realized it back at the house, but when I felt I was being watched from the trees, I must have been sensing her presence. I rather feel that she drove me to kill Mother, that without the little girl's interference I would never have reached this point. Still, I cannot blame her, even though I should. She has twisted my mind to such a degree that I can now only see the world from her point of view.

"When you're ready," the warden calls out from the far side of the room.

I hear footsteps walking to the far wall.

Closing my eyes, I prepare for death. If there is any life beyond this one, I feel certain that after the brief pain I experience while dying, I shall find myself back at the house. I also believe that Father, who they tell me was executed last week, will be there too.

Suddenly I feel something touching my left hand. Little fingers link with mine and squeeze my hand tight. It's Annie, the first Annie, and as soon as her flesh touches mine I feel an overwhelming sense of love bursting through my soul. She's neither cruel nor vindictive, and she's certainly not evil. She just wants a family.

The last thing I hear is the sound of the lever being pulled, and the last thing I feel is a massive surge of power that bursts through my body and escapes from my lips as a dying gasp. And then comes the vast dark emptiness of death.

EPILOGUE

I HEAR THE CAR before I see it. There's an engine somewhere beyond the trees, and sure enough a red sports car comes into view a moment later. By the time it pulls up in the driveway, I can already see who's inside.

"Well hello there!" Harriet Roland coos as she gets out of the car, waving at me and grinning. "How are you doing there, neighbor? Do I spy a young lady who's finally out of those horrendous plaster casts?"

Having spent the morning sitting on the porch steps, patiently transplanting spinach seeds into their new pots, I'm somewhat taken aback by the sudden arrivals. Still, I wipe my hands on the sides of my jeans and get to my feet, while forcing a smile. I know it's important to present a calm face to the world, to show good character, and I figure it should be pretty easy to make Harriet and her daughter think that everything is okay.

"Oh my God!" Harriet continues. "Look at you,

Annie! Up and about, and out of those wretched plaster casts already." She turns to Tabitha, who's a little slower getting out of the car. "Look, darling! Annie's all better!"

Tabitha smiles at me, but there's a hint of concern in her eyes. If I didn't know better, I'd be worried.

"I'm sorry we haven't been out sooner," Harriet continues, shaking my hand enthusiastically, "but we were away for the summer, visiting our house by the beach. You know how it is, you go out there intending to spend a week or two, and then before you know it the summer is almost over and you wonder where all the time went!"

"Sure," I reply, smiling cautiously as Tabitha comes over to join us.

"Do they hurt?" Harriet asks.

"I'm sorry?"

"Your legs. Do they still hurt?"

"Oh..." I pause, before looking down at my legs. There are a couple of scars still, but considering how badly they were damaged, I figure that's not too bad. "No. No, my legs are fine now. A little stiff still, but that'll pass."

"How wonderful," she continues. "When we came before, I felt so sorry for you, stuck up there in that little bedroom. The summer was so glorious, it was such rotten luck for you that you had to miss most of it. Why, you must be -"

Stopping suddenly, she seems to have spotted something nearby. Turning, I realize what's wrong. Scott is on the far side of the porch, slumped over slightly in his wheelchair. For someone who doesn't know what happened, he's probably an alarming sight.

"Is..." Harriet pauses, with obvious concern in her voice. "Is that your darling little brother?"

"It is," I reply, smiling as I watch Scott for a moment, before ridding my face of the smile and turning back to Harriet. "I'm afraid he had an accident. He's fine physically, but mentally... We don't know if he'll ever talk again. All he does is sit in that chair and stare into space. The doctors say a blow to the back of the head like that can cause lasting damage, but at least he's not in pain, not as far as we can tell."

"How awful," Harriet replies, with tears in her eyes. "Do you mind if I ask what happened?"

"It's a little sensitive, actually," I tell her. "For his sake, we prefer not to talk about it too much. We don't really know whether he can hear us, and we don't want to upset him. Would you like to come inside, by the way? I can make some tea or coffee for you."

"That would be lovely," Harriet replies, as she and Tabitha follow me to the steps. "Is your mother not in?"

"No, not really," I reply, glancing at the basement door as I step into the kitchen. "Sorry, she's away for a while. I don't know if... I mean, I don't know when she'll be back."

"I hope no-one else is sick," Harriet says, with obvious concern. "It seems your family has had such terrible luck lately."

"My aunt's not well, actually." I fill the water-boiler and flick a switch on the side, before turning to her. "She's -"

I pause for a moment as I see that while Harriet and Tabitha are smiling at me as if nothing's wrong, there's another figure standing nearby. It's little Annie, the first Annie, the rotten little girl who, according to my research, lived in this house more than one hundred and fifty years ago and drowned in the lake. When I thought Annie Garrett was haunting this house, I was wrong; the ghosts were Annie Garrett's mother, who trying to warn me, and little Annie Shaw, the first Annie. Even now, drips of water are running down Annie Shaw's rotten legs and falling onto the floor. She's the one who started this whole thing, the one who has been waiting ever since for a chance to experience the childhood she missed, the one who wanted nothing more than the love of a father. She haunted Annie Garrett, trying to experience life through her, but Annie Garrett became a twisted monster. Annie Shaw is finally happy now, though; she gets to feel everything I feel, she gets to experience real love through me, and it's all she's ever wanted.

Sometimes I hear a whisper in my head, guiding me, but I don't mind. I can barely remember what it was like before we came to this house.

"My mother has gone to look after my aunt," I continue, regathering my composure and turning back to Harriet. "She really might be quite some time. Again, it's a difficult situation."

"Oh, that's too bad," Harriet replies, "but at least you're here to hold the fort."

I nod, unable to keep from grinning with pure

pride.

Next to Harriet, Tabitha is staring at me with a hint of concern. It's tempting to believe that she suspects something, but of course that would be impossible. She's just some dumb kid, there's no way she could ever come close to guessing the truth about everything that has happened in this house. Maybe she senses that I'm a little different, but it's not exactly a crime to change over the course of a long, hot summer.

"I'm sure your mother is very proud of you for taking on all these responsibilities," Harriet continues. "I know it's a lot for a girl your age, but this whole house looks absolutely spotless. I'm almost tempted to say that it seems better than the first time we came over, but of course back then you were still unpacking. Still, your parents must be so proud of you, the way you've stepped up to the plate and taken over."

"Yes," I reply, as the water-boiler starts to whistle, "they *are* proud." I pause for a moment. "Especially Dad."

"And of course Tabitha and I can chip in," she adds. "We'll come over and -"

"No," I say firmly.

"We -" She frowns, as if she thinks maybe she misheard. "I'm sorry?"

"It's very kind of you to offer," I continue, realizing that I need to stand my ground, "but I can't possibly accept. We're fine, and we don't need your help."

"But -"

"Please don't come here again," I add. "I'd hate

to have to report you for trespassing."

***

Once Harriet and Tabitha have left, I spend a little while tidying the kitchen before setting dinner on to cook. I'm using a new recipe, one that's very complex, so I put the whole thing on a low heat, figuring that the flavors will be stronger that way. Besides, there's no need to hurry.

The dead Annie watches, of course. She can feel everything I feel, but she still likes to be in the room with me, and I don't mind her presence at all. It's good to have a little company, even if she never says anything. She just stands, dripping, staring at me with her rotten face, feeling every emotion that I feel. In a strange way, her presence is almost calming, but I think maybe that's something she does on purpose. She guides me constantly.

"Here you go," I say to Scott as I head out onto the porch. Crouching in front of him, I dip a spoon into the bowl of porridge and then slip a mouthful between his lips. He doesn't really respond much, but when I push the spoon further back his gag reflex kicks in.

His eyes stare back at me. Sometimes I wonder how much he remembers about that night.

"It's better this way," I tell him with a smile. "Annie attracted us to this house for a reason. She had it all planned out, she reached out and found another Annie to live here. Sometimes I even think she caused my accident, so she could get what she wanted. You'll see, we can be happy here. Truly happy, but..."

I pause for a moment, spotting a figure on the lawn. Annie Garrett's mother is still around, but I manage to ignore her and she stays well away from the house. She seems so lost, and sometimes I think I should try to find her body so she can be set free. Maybe then she can go and join her husband and daughter, wherever they ended up after they were executed. One thing's certain: Annie Garrett's ghost was never here. Just the other Annie. Little Annie.

"We just can't let the outside world know," I continue, turning back to Scott. "They'd see how close we are to Dad, and they'd think awful, dark things. They wouldn't understand that it's pure, that it's just a spiritual connection. There's nothing physical going on, that would be wrong, it would go against everything that the first Annie wants. She just needs to feel loved and happy, and through us... well, mainly through me, she gets that."

I wait for a reply, but of course none comes. Sometimes I think I see a hint of resentment in his eyes, but I'm probably imagining that. Besides, every time I start to doubt myself, or I start to wonder if maybe this whole situation is wrong, I feel that whisper in my head again, setting me back on course. It's as if the first Annie knows exactly how to calm all my fears.

"Dad loves you, you know," I continue, hoping for a flicker of recognition on Scott's face. "We have the perfect life here, there's no need to think about anything else. You'll see."

It takes a few more minutes to feed him, and all the while he simply stares at me, his eyes filled with a kind of blank horror.

"That's good," I tell him finally, getting to my feet. "You're doing so well these days. I know you saw a lot that night, and I know some of it might still not make a whole lot of sense, but..." I pause for a moment, watching the faint twitch in his eyes. The truth is, Scott hasn't been the same since the night when the first Annie came back, and personally I think his mind is pretty much shot to pieces. Maybe professional help would be able to fix him, but it's not like we can afford to have the authorities looking into things. Besides, it's not a huge problem; whenever I feel myself worrying about him, the first Annie reaches into my mind and makes everything feels okay again.

I leave Scott on the porch as I head inside. I should probably take some food down to Mom too, but lately I've been feeling less keen on her. Again, I guess that's the first Annie's influence. Maybe I'll start feeding Mom every *other* day, rather than every day. I'm sure she'll be fine. At the same time, sometimes I wonder...

Turning, I see that the dead little girl has come a little closer.

My thoughts about my mother instantly start fading.

She'll be fine down there.

Realizing that I have more important matters to deal with, I head through to the hallway and then I start making my way upstairs. The other Annie follows, as always; she likes to keep close, so she can share every moment of my experience. After all, it took so long for everything in this house to be perfect, and I don't blame her for wanting to enjoy herself. Stopping at the door near the top of the stairs, I look down at the words 'Annie's room' carved into the wood, and I can't help but smile. I remember when I felt trapped in the room, and there were times when I felt I'd never get out.

Now I can't wait to get back up here each day, to experience pure and total joy, and to know that this joy is shared by others. Father is sleeping in his own room, which is how things should be. I'll wake him for dinner later.

Trembling with anticipation, I turn the handle and open the door to my room, and then I step inside. Dinner is cooking slowly and I have time to rest for a few minutes, so I sit on the edge of my bed and start removing my shoes. The house is calm and quiet, and I'm ahead with all my chores for the day. We have the perfect family, and Dad's so proud of me, sometimes I just want to burst with happiness. Other people probably wouldn't understand the way we live, they'd probably come up with filthy assumptions, but they'd be so utterly wrong, it's laughable. Closing my eyes, I take a deep breath and savor the moment. A few seconds later, I realize I can hear faint drips falling onto the floorboards, and I smile.

Behind me, the door swings shut.

Also by Amy Cross

The Curse of Wetherley House

"If you walk through that door, Evil Mary will get you."

When she agrees to visit a supposedly haunted house with an old friend, Rosie assumes she'll encounter nothing more scary than a few creaks and bumps in the night. Even the legend of Evil Mary doesn't put her off. After all, she knows ghosts aren't real. But when Mary makes her first appearance, Rosie realizes she might already be trapped.

For more than a century, Wetherley House has been cursed. A horrific encounter on a remote road in the late 1800's has already caused a chain of misery and pain for all those who live at the house. Wetherley House was abandoned long ago, after a terrible discovery in the basement, something has remained undetected within its room. And even the local children know that Evil Mary waits in the house for anyone foolish enough to walk through the front door.

Before long, Rosie realizes that her entire life has been defined by the spirit of a woman who died in agony. Can she become the first person to escape Evil Mary, or will she fall victim to the same fate as the house's other occupants?

Also by Amy Cross

The Ghosts of Hexley Airport

Ten years ago, more than two hundred people died in a horrific plane crash at Hexley Airport.

Today, some say their ghosts still haunt the terminal building.

When she starts her new job at the airport, working a night shift as part of the security team, Casey assumes the stories about the place can't be true. Even when she has a strange encounter in a deserted part of the departure hall, she's certain that ghosts aren't real.

Soon, however, she's forced to face the truth. Not only is there something haunting the airport's buildings and tarmac, but a sinister force is working behind the scenes to replicate the circumstances of the original accident. And as a snowstorm moves in, Hexley Airport looks set to witness yet another disaster.

Printed in Poland
by Amazon Fulfillment
Poland Sp. z o.o., Wrocław